THREE DOG KNIGHT

MIDNIGHT EMPIRE: THE TOWER, BOOK 2

ANNABEL CHASE

RED PALM PRESS LLC

Copyright © 2021 by Annabel Chase

All rights reserved.

No part of this book may be reproduced in any form or by any electronic or mechanical means, including information storage and retrieval systems, without written permission from the author, except for the use of brief quotations in a book review.

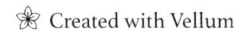

❦ Created with Vellum

PROLOGUE

Henry stretched his arms over his head. His back was already sore and it wasn't even midday. His wife wanted him to take care, but what choice did he have? The work was hard and the house was enormous, but that meant it took time and during that time Henry could feed his family. He was no stranger to hard work.

"Another delivery's coming from the quarry today," Geoffrey said.

"Good because we're almost through the last batch of stones."

Geoffrey seemed to know everything even though he was only a laborer like Henry. There was something different about Geoffrey. His hazel eyes shone a touch too bright and solid muscles bulged beneath his clothes. He'd once rolled up his sleeves on an unseasonably warm day and Henry had marveled at the excessive hair on his arms. Henry had heard tales of people with their bodies covered in a layer of dark fuzz, but they came from the Mediterranean and Geoffrey had been born in Britain, same as

Henry. Geoffrey's parents were called Mary and George, hardly names he associated with foreigners.

"Not good," Anthony complained. "I was hoping for a break. Now we've no excuse but to keep working."

Henry lifted a stone and wedged it into place. This would be a fine wall once it was finished. He was proud of the fruits of his labor, however hard on his back and shoulders. Even his knees seemed to groan from the constant strain of lifting and turning.

"If you get to keep working, you get to keep eating," Henry reminded them.

"Speaking of eating," Geoffrey said, grinning.

Henry and Anthony laughed. Geoffrey ate more than any man Henry had ever met. That likely accounted for the muscles. Henry wasn't sure how his friend managed to acquire so much food. It probably helped that Geoffrey had no wife or kids to feed. More for him.

Henry and Anthony continued to work while Geoffrey disappeared into the nearby woods. Hopefully no one would see him disappear and make a fuss. He seemed to be very good at moving unnoticed. Not Henry. Henry's pale skin flashed like a beacon wherever he went.

"This will make a very fine house once it's finished," Anthony remarked. He took a step back to admire the foundation and the start of the fourth and final wall. "What do you suppose it'd be like to live in a house like this?"

"Drafty," Henry replied and they both laughed.

The sound of wheels grinding against gravel drew their attention to the arrival of more supplies.

Henry winced at the wagon teeming with rocks. "I know we need more, but my arms ache just looking at them." More than once his fatigue had caused him to fall asleep before supper. His wife had been less than impressed by his stamina.

Anthony reached for a stone at the top of the pile. "I wish all of them were this size."

The chosen stone was the size of Henry's foot. He shook his head. "Not me. It would only take longer. Bigger stones take up more space."

As Henry turned his attention to the mortar mix, Anthony secured the stone in place.

"This one's marked up," Henry said, noticing deep grooves in the small stone. "Do you think anyone will see?"

Anthony shrugged. "Too small. I'd chance it."

Henry cast a wary glance at the stone. "What if it's not as hard as the others and that's why it's all marked up? Might be too weak to be part of the wall."

Anthony contemplated the stone. "Too late now." His mouth split. "Maybe if our work was shoddier, it would be worth removing."

No chance of that. Henry took too much pride in his work. They all did, except maybe Kenneth who seemed to prefer napping to working.

"Geoffrey's headed back. Just in time too." Anthony glanced over his shoulder as another man crossed the grounds toward them. The master builder.

Henry signaled to Geoffrey to hurry. The burly man was a hard worker and Henry didn't want to lose him. He also told good stories which Henry appreciated—stories about fairies and elves and times long past. If nothing else, he made the work go faster.

As Geoffrey neared the site, his body began to twitch and he nearly toppled over. Henry frowned. He'd never seen anyone have a fit before, although his wife had made sympathetic noises about a neighbor with such an affliction.

Geoffrey's body went rigid and Henry worried he'd fall flat on his face. What happened next, however, was much worse.

A monster erupted from Geoffrey's bright-eyed and bulky body. Coarse hair coated taut muscles from head to toe. With pointed ears and an elongated snout, the head resembled that of a wolf, except this creature was standing on its hind legs and was much more than a wolf.

All the air escaped Henry's lungs.

Anthony hugged a stone to his chest, his jaw slack. Nobody moved.

The monster looked at its paws as though perplexed by its own appearance.

Henry wasn't sure who cast the first stone. He assumed it was Anthony, who stood closest to the pile of rocks. A sizable chunk of earth whizzed through the air and pelted the monster in the gut. The creature roared and the sound deafened Henry's ears. He'd never heard a noise like that in his life and hoped never to hear it again.

Stones rained down on the creature as the men came to their senses and used the only weapon within their grasp that allowed them to keep their distance. Henry couldn't bring himself to throw a stone. He stood against the half-built wall, terror winding its way through his body. It started in his lungs and spread to his heart before inching through the rest of his organs and extremities like a worm through an apple. He opened his mouth to shout, to beg the monster for mercy, but no sound came out.

The creature tore through the men like they were weeds from the garden. Henry ducked as a body flew over his head and slammed into the stone wall behind him and he was pleased to see the wall held. Henry was awestruck by the sheer strength of the beast. No wonder Geoffrey had always seemed fresh and rested at the end of a long day. The monster within must have given him unimaginable power.

Henry remained rooted in place, unable to move his legs in order to flee. A blessing in disguise, he thought. He knew what happened to animals that ran—they became prey and Henry didn't want to be any creature's prey.

The monster ripped an arm from its socket, flung it over his shoulder like a discarded apple core, and came to an abrupt halt. His head jerked to the side as though wrenched by an invisible hand. The fur on its face receded and then returned.

Henry blinked, uncertain what was happening. The creature seemed to be stuck between its two forms, alternating between monster features and human features. Relief flooded Henry's body. It was too late for the dead men around them, but it wasn't too late for Henry.

The jaw softened and shortened and finally Geoffrey's face emerged. "Help," the creature said, although the word sounded slightly garbled to Henry's ears. There was no shine left in the eyes. They fixed on Henry, dull and flat.

Henry observed the carnage around him, feeling rattled and confused. Help him? He'd just slaughtered a dozen men.

And yet Henry felt a wave of compassion wash over him. He peeled himself away from the wall, deliberating.

Geoffrey dropped to his knees. Henry winced at the sound of bones cracking. Geoffrey's clothes were in tatters and Henry could still see tufts of fur dotting his exposed skin. He seized and collapsed on his side.

Henry inched toward him. Nearby was a large rock that someone had thrown in vain during the height of the monster's tirade. Geoffrey had no wife or children. Henry could stop this now. With one eye trained on the twitching creature, Henry retrieved the rock. He raised it over his head and brought it down on the creature's head with as much force as he could muster. He wasn't ashamed to say—when he told the story later—that he closed his eyes, unable to witness his own actions. The monster had been part of Geoffrey somehow and Henry had liked the man.

Except he wasn't a man at all.

Geoffrey stopped moving and grew quiet. Henry waited a few minutes to see if the creature stirred again, pretending not to see the blood that pooled beneath the creature's head. Henry was aware when his heartbeat slowed to normal. He looked back at the house and wondered what he would tell the owner. There would be delays. It couldn't be helped. He hoped the house didn't gain a reputation for being cursed. The owner might decide to abandon the work and Henry would be out of a job.

His gaze shifted to the body at his feet. At least the worst part was over now. He'd gotten to Geoffrey in time.

There would be no more monsters.

1

The view from Hampstead Heath was deceptive. Lights blazed in the distance. They signaled security. Safety. Like I said—deceptive.

"Avoid the water," I advised. "There might be a parasitic demon in it."

Kami cast a glance at the pond. "If there isn't a demon, there's definitely some other kind of parasite I don't want any part of. Can you believe people actually used to swim in that mud hole?"

Once upon a time Hampstead Heath was the largest park in Britannia City. That was before the Great Eruption when ten of the world's supervolcanoes threw a party at the same time. They invited all the monsters they'd been hiding and triggered the Eternal Night because sunlight couldn't penetrate the thick layer of volcanic ash in the atmosphere. Vampires eventually seized power and Hampstead Heath was overrun by creatures great and small. Residents avoided the area if they could help it. Whereas Hyde Park and Regent's Park adapted to the changes, Hampstead Heath succumbed to it like the Titanic to an iceberg.

"Seems quiet here. What exactly are we looking for?" I asked.

"The complaint wasn't very specific. That's why I said to load up on weapons." Kami inclined her head in my direction. "And you apparently chose to ignore the directive. I only see Babe."

I sliced the air with my beloved axe. "I thought you just wanted an excuse to test out the new crossbow."

Kamikaze Marwin loved weapons the way vampires loved blood. The stocky blonde relished the way they felt in her hand, their sound when they made contact with their intended target, and the damage they could inflict. I discovered this fact about her very early in our friendship when we were two frightened teenaged orphans fighting to survive in the tunnels of Britannia City. If there was a discarded piece of metal or a scrap of rubber, rest assured Kami found a way to weaponize it. Now she acted as the banner's resident expert. If there was a new weapon making the rounds, she'd hunt it down and master it before the rest of the knights managed to learn its name.

She patted the strap of the new crossbow. "That may have been an added incentive."

I peered at the expanse of darkness. "If they'd invest in more lights in the park, they might reduce the number of threats."

"Or they could try a ward."

"That's too tricky. They'd end up keeping everybody out."

Kami shrugged. "Seems like that's the end result anyway."

A flash of movement close to the ground caught my eye. "On your left."

"Saw it." Kami's voice dropped to a whisper. "What are you thinking?"

"Not sure. Too small to be anything significant."

She cast me a sidelong glance. "Can you win it over?"

I reached out with my mind and tried to latch on to the nearest creature.

"Anything?" Kami prompted.

"Nothing noteworthy. Pretty sure it's a rat." And you couldn't swing a cat in this city without hitting a rat the size of a feral hog. Vampires and rats were the clear winners of the Eternal Night.

"Let's talk to the client," Kami suggested. "Maybe he can give us more details."

Gerald Latham lived nearby, hence his cry for help. According to Gerald, he'd requested help from his landlord, but the plea was summarily dismissed. Mitchell Dansker owned half the buildings between Hampstead Heath and Hampstead Village, as well as a smattering of other buildings gifted to the vampire by House Lewis as a show of gratitude for helping the royal vampire family secure the city during the Battle of Britannia. It seemed that Dansker liked owning properties more than he liked caring for those who resided in them. Thanks to a community fund request, Gerald scraped together enough money to pay our fee. Given the lengths he went to, I wanted to take his complaint seriously, but I was beginning to wonder whether Dansker was right to ignore the request. Just because the vampire had a reputation for callousness didn't mean his decision was a bad one. Even a stopped clock was right twice a day.

The avenue of houses between the Heath and the Village were once grand historic homes worth millions of pounds when the city was still known as London. Gerald Latham lived in a ground-floor flat of one such house—a detached Edwardian—and the rest of the 7500-square-foot house was occupied by two other families. It was the kind of house my mother would've stopped to admire and then regaled me with facts about its construction and likely inhabitants prior to the Eternal Night.

Looking at the red brick facade, I felt a pang of loss. My mother had been a bright spark whose light still managed to influence my daily life.

Kami rang the buzzer for Gerald's flat. Minutes stretched as we awaited a response. Finally the front door opened and a craggy face appeared.

"I didn't hire you to fight the critters here. You're supposed to be out there." He jerked his chin toward the park.

Kami simply smiled. "Gerald Latham, I presume?"

"No, I'm the queen. Who the bloody hell do you think I am?"

I tried a friendly smile. "Mr. Latham, may we come in? We'd like to ask you a few questions that would help us complete our assignment."

He shook his head. "Women. Always needing more. I knew I should've hired a knight from a regular banner, but they were more expensive." He yanked open the door. "Come in, but wipe your feet. If you've been traipsing through the park, you'll bring the mud with you."

Kami and I exchanged glances and each took a turn wiping our feet on the doormat.

Well, this would be fun.

Despite the interior changes, the house managed to retain its charm. There were gleaming wooden floors and a set of curved windows at the front that filled my heart with the kind of joy usually reserved for animals and chocolate.

"Grade II Listed?" I asked.

Gerald looked at me with keen interest. "Heard of that, have you?"

"My mother was a history teacher."

"Usually I'd moan about vampires changing everything, but I'm glad they got rid of them listings or else I wouldn't be able to live in a place like this." He glanced upward, presumably to admire the cornices on the ceiling since that was the only detail worth ogling. "The landlord is rotten in plenty of ways, but he keeps this building looking spiffy."

"We need to know about the creatures," Kami said. "We did a brief survey of the park, but all we saw were rats."

Gerald tugged his earlobe. "Exactly."

I peered at him. "Exactly what?"

"Rats. They're infesting the whole area. Any minute we're going to get a new plague and you'll know where it originated." He jabbed an angry finger in the direction of the park.

"Mr. Latham, you don't hire a knight because of rats," Kami explained. "They're a regular feature of city life."

"But they've been digging in my rubbish bins," he objected.

Kami sighed. "They're rats. That's what they do."

"They haven't bothered with the bins until recently. They're growing bolder every day, the bastards." Gerald folded his arms and scowled. "I should enjoy a reasonable expectation of privacy. I can't do that if I have to worry about rats invading my space."

"If you've thrown something away in the bin, doesn't that mean you no longer want it?" Kami asked. "Why would you expect any privacy in something you don't own anymore?"

He scoffed. "What do they teach knights nowadays? You two know nothing about the law."

"We're not adjudicators," I reminded him.

"Get rid of them rats. That's what I'm paying you for."

Kami blew stray hairs out of her eye. "Technically you haven't paid us anything yet."

"And I won't if you don't take care of them rats. I'm tired of finding my bins knocked over and dragged halfway down the street. Mrs. Lundy found a letter I'd discarded and she's four houses down. Read it from start to finish, too, the nosy thing. It's not just the rubbish either. My upstairs neighbor has a baby and she's afraid to take the boy out in the pram."

One of his comments stayed with me. "You mentioned they only started digging in the bins recently. Did anything change, like maybe you're using a new type of bin?"

His scowl intensified. "Blame the victim, is that it?"

"No, Mr. Latham. I'm only trying to help. There've always been rats in the park and if they haven't been this much of a nuisance before, there has to be a reason why that's changed, right?"

He hesitated. "I suppose."

Look at me making sense notwithstanding my lady parts. Gold star.

"If you can think of anything that's different…" I began.

He ran his tongue along the front of his teeth, a habit I detested. "There's a new family moved in next door a couple weeks ago. Maybe they're drawing the rats closer to the neighborhood."

"Why would a new family attract rats?" Kami asked. "This street is full of flats. You must have people moving in and out all the time."

His face hardened. "Because they're vampires, that's why."

Ah. I was beginning to grasp the true reason for Gerald Latham's complaint.

"Mr. Latham, I can understand why you're not overjoyed

having vampires as neighbors, but last I checked, vampires don't attract vermin," I said.

Kami's face grew flushed as the realization hit her, too. "What did you think would happen? We'd march next door and rough them up for you? Scare them out of the neighborhood? That's not what we do."

"You knights have a certain reputation. I only want you to make it clear what will happen if they make trouble for the rest of us."

I blew out a breath. "They have every right to live here, same as you."

He balled his hands into fists. "Not the same as me. They occupy most of the city. This street may be owned by one, but the rest of us are good people who don't need the threat of vampires in our own backyards. My other neighbors upstairs—their girl Kari even ran off after the vamps moved in. I guarantee it was because of the son. That boy has trouble written all over him."

In Gerald's mind, it wasn't really that his expectation of privacy had been violated. It was that his sense of security was under threat. His home was his castle and that castle now had a moat filled with alligators.

"Have the rats really been attacking the bins?" I asked.

"Yes," he bellowed. "And if you're not going to do anything about them, you can take your leave." He ushered us toward the door. "Next time I'll gather the extra coin and hire a real knight." He glared at us for good measure before slamming the door.

Kami and I stood on the doorstep in a stupor.

"Which reputation of ours do you think he was referring to?" she finally asked.

"Not the violent one. If we were as violent as everyone claims, we'd be thrilled to blow up a bunch of rats and rough up a vampire family." I glanced down the quiet street. "To be fair, I feel like most people feel that way, even the ones without violent tendencies."

There was no love lost between me and rats. I'd endured more than my share of them as a teenager. Even so, I had no interest in wasting valuable time and resources protecting Mr. Latham's garbage and pushing his bigoted agenda.

"Why don't we at least take a look at the bins while we're here?" I suggested. "Maybe we'll notice something unusual."

"Good idea. He did say the issues only started recently, so it could be down to something he's overlooked."

I eyed the house next door. "Because he's been too busy looking at the neighbors as the cause."

We ambled around the corner to the alley between the two houses where the bins were located. There were three sets of green bins on one side and only one bin on the other. I wondered whether Dansker displaced any human tenants to make room for one vampire family.

The row of bins began to shake and Kami and I drew to a halt.

A creature exploded from behind the bins. The containers shot in all directions like oversized shrapnel and the contents followed suit. The stench alone was enough to knock me off my feet. Wet noodles slapped my face. I spit one out of my mouth and focused on the creature looming in front of us.

A fox.

Not the kind of regular fox I occasionally saw slinking down an alley. This one was larger and more substantial. Like the oversized rats, this one seemed to be on steroids.

It wasn't the rats messing with Gerald's beloved rubbish. It was this guy.

Kami aimed her crossbow at the fox.

I scrambled between them. "No, don't!"

The fox saw an opportunity and took off.

Kami lowered her crossbow. "I wasn't planning to kill it. I only wanted to scare it away."

I glanced in the direction of the retreating fox. "Mission accomplished."

Kami stared at the mess. "That thing was big, right?"

"It wasn't small."

"What's going on here?" a voice demanded.

I turned to see a couple watching us with a mixture of interest and revulsion.

"You live here?" Kami asked. She pulled a noodle from her hair and tossed it on the ground.

"Upstairs." The man pointed to the flat above Gerald's.

"You have the missing daughter," I said.

"She isn't missing. She just ran off," the man said. "She'll come back when she's tired of being cold and hungry." He slung an arm around his wife's shoulders and squeezed. "Isn't that right?"

The woman nodded, but I could see a question in her dark eyes.

"Do you think something happened between her and the vampire boy next door?" I asked.

They seemed equally astonished by the question. "We haven't even met them," the man said. "Kari's been upset about other things. Teenage girl drama. I'm sure you know all about that."

Kami and I remained quiet. Our teenage drama would have been remarkably different from someone like Kari who had two parents and a roof over her head.

"If she doesn't come home, feel free to contact us." I produced a business card and handed it to the mother, but the father intercepted it.

"Thank you, but I have every confidence she'll arrive back home within the week." He tucked the card into his pocket and I had no doubt I'd never hear from them whether Kari came home or not.

"Have you noticed a problem with rats encroaching on your territory?" I asked.

"Did Mr. Latham call you?" The man laughed. "I swear he gets more paranoid every day."

"Yes, we've noticed it," the woman said. "But this is the city. There are always going to be rats."

"And foxes," Kami added.

The woman shot her a quizzical look. "We had foxes in the rubbish, too?"

"What do you think caused this mess?" I asked.

"Don't worry," Kami said. "We just scared one half to death, so I doubt it will come back to bother you."

"Did you wound it?" the woman asked.

"We don't kill defenseless animals if that's what you're asking," I said. "We told Mr. Latham the same thing. It just seemed hungry and frightened."

The man glanced at his wife. "I'll set traps. I don't want to risk you getting attacked if you come out here alone."

"Honestly, you're better off securing your bins," I told them. "That's the temptation. If you take that away, they have less reason to be so close to the house."

He nodded. "Thanks for the tip. I assume part of your service includes cleaning up the mess you make?"

Kami opened her mouth with what I knew would be a smart remark, so I shook my head at her. It wouldn't take us long to clean this up. I had the feeling if we didn't, his wife would be the one out here on her hands and knees.

"We'll take care of it," I promised.

He maneuvered his wife around the corner of the house toward the front door.

Once we finished the thankless task, Kami looked at me and smiled through the muck on her face. "I could use a drink after this."

"I don't think there's a pub in the city that would be willing to have us in this condition." Not even Hole, which was exactly as its name suggested.

"The Crown then. Simon won't mind. His clientele are almost all shifters anyway."

I snorted. "I dare you to suggest that shifters smell in the middle of the pub. I'll be the one in the corner belly laughing."

Kami nudged me with her elbow. "No, you wouldn't. You'd have my back."

I would. Kami was my best friend and I'd protect her no matter how many shifters she knowingly insulted. It was part of our unwritten pact that we made as teenagers. In this world of darkness and uncertainty, at least we knew we could count on each other.

2

The Crown was located near the Circus, where the Knights of Boudica were headquartered. The pub was one of the few buildings in the neighborhood that managed to retain its original stained-glass windows. Instead of dark brown walls, they were painted an off-white to make the interior appear bigger and brighter. Light spilled from the strings of lights that clung to the ceiling, bathing the room in a pale yellow glow.

Simon waved to us from behind the bar as we entered. As a werewolf, he catered to the shapeshifter crowd. We were regulars, though, and Simon treated us like royalty. He liked having knights on hand because we could act as peacekeepers when his patrons got out of hand, as shifters were wont to do. More than once I'd found myself holding back one werewolf while Kami held back his opponent. Funny thing about werewolves. They didn't love to be strong-armed by two women and tended to flee the premises immediately afterward.

The large oval table at the back was usually reserved for us, but it was currently occupied by a group of werewolves.

It was only Kami and I tonight, though. We took one of the smaller tables without complaint.

I sniffed the air. "Usually this place smells like damp fur, but all I can smell is us."

"How bad is it? Because I spot a few rather attractive male specimens," Kami said. A pitcher of ale sat between us and Simon had thoughtfully delivered two damp cloths as well so we could clean ourselves up in the restroom.

"Even if they're nasally-challenged, I don't think you're going to attract anybody while you have pesto ground into your scalp."

Kami touched her scalp and grimaced. "Why didn't you tell me I missed a spot?"

"Because I figured you'd wash it out when you shower tonight. No harm done. I hear pesto is an excellent moisturizer."

"You're hilarious. Maybe we should call your boyfriend and ask him to meet us here. See what he thinks of your eau de rubbish scent."

My fingers curled around my glass. "He's not my boyfriend."

Kami blew a raspberry. "Oh, please. I haven't seen you this enamored since...Well, never."

"That assignment is over and done with. I'll never see him again." Which was a good thing, too, because the more interaction I had with vampires, the greater the risk to my life. As a dhampir—the offspring of a witch and a vampire—I was the one species vampires feared. Vampires were immortal not invulnerable; they could still be killed. Like sunlight, a dhampir could kill them with minimal effort. Once the sun was no longer an obstacle, vampires focused on eradicating their other major threat. Thanks to my mother's intensive training, I learned to conceal my true nature. There was always the chance of discovery, though.

Always.

Kami smiled. "Somehow I doubt you'll never see him again. There were too many hormones working overtime."

"I'm thirty, not thirteen. Besides, he's a prince *and* a vampire. Both of those facts make a relationship with him a nonstarter."

She pounded a fist on the table. "Aha! So you admit you've considered it."

"I admit nothing." Just because we'd fought together to rescue his sister and recover a powerful stone with elemental powers didn't mean we'd formed a connection.

Nope. No connection at all.

"You two are rather spirited this evening," Simon said as he passed by with another round for the table at the back.

"Not as spirited as those guys," I said. The werewolves seemed to grow louder by the minute.

His gaze flicked to the large table. "I'll cut them off before they get too rowdy."

"Let's hope so," Kami said. "We already cleaned up one mess tonight."

"I think you'll find *I* cleaned up the mess."

"And I held the bins in place so they didn't tip over. Team effort." She held out her fist for me to bump it.

Simon chuckled and carried on.

As Kami and I finished the last of our pitcher, the voices around us grew deeper and louder. At one point I glanced at the bar to see Simon's gaze fixed on the oval table. I got the sense he was uneasy about whatever storm was brewing between the werewolves.

Kami twisted to observe the pack. "I can't tell what they're getting worked up about."

I lowered my voice. "Does it matter? If they don't calm down soon, the paws and claws will be out." And our night will be ruined.

Simon seemed to be on the same page. "You know the rules, fellas," he called to them. "No fur in my pub or you're banished."

A broad-shouldered werewolf held up his hands in acquiescence. "Wouldn't dream of it, mate. We're just having a laugh."

Not all of them. Two of them were glowering at each other and I heard a low growl. I didn't like the sudden shift in energy.

"We should go," I said.

Kami signaled to Simon for the bill.

"What's wrong with you tonight?" a werewolf thundered. "Stop twitching."

A chair flew across the table and smashed against the wall. Kami and I sprang to our feet at the same time.

Patrons scrambled for the door. They weren't fools. An entire table of angry werewolves could get ugly fast.

"That's enough, fellas," Simon ordered. "Last warning."

The warning fell on deaf ears. Two werewolves were at each other's throats, literally. Each one had a hand wrapped around the other's throat. We needed to separate them. Now.

"Donnie, settle down," one of the other werewolves urged. "You don't seem like yourself."

I didn't know Donnie, but his friend was right. The werewolf even looked strange, like his human face had started to transform and stopped midway.

"Harry, let Donnie go and then he'll do the same. Nice and easy," another werewolf said in an encouraging voice.

Harry let go.

Donnie responded by lifting Harry over his head with both hands, preparing to launch the poor guy across the room.

I jumped on my table and vaulted into the air, grabbing a string of ceiling lights with both hands. I used the momentum to swing across the large table. The heels of my boots landed squarely on Donnie's chest and he sailed backward, hitting the wall with arms and legs spread like a starfish. Harry slammed against the wall over his friend's head and fell to the floor with a thud.

A hush fell over the pub.

I watched Donnie, hoping he'd come to his senses.

"Are you going to behave now?" I prompted.

Fabric shred and fur sprouted as both men unleashed the beasts within. They were terrifying creatures that hovered somewhere between man and wolf.

"I think that's a no," Kami said behind me.

I felt a rush of remorse. I was trying to knock sense into Donnie, not escalate matters.

Donnie towered over Harry even in wolf form. They stood on their hind legs, their bodies wrapped in corded muscle and covered in patchy fur. Their muzzles were more lupine than human but their blurred nature made them appear even more monstrous. These two would never be confused with actual wolves in the forest.

Harry seemed perplexed, studying his paws as though he'd never seen them before.

Donnie released a roar at the crowd that sent shivers down my spine. It wasn't so much fear as an instinctive response to a primal sound. I quickly collected myself. Donnie was big and furry, but I'd fought bigger and furrier and lived to tell the tale.

"Looks like Donnie don't want to drink here no more," one of the werewolves muttered.

Simon climbed on top of the bar wielding a stun gun shaped like a wand. "I'm warning you lot right now. Nobody else turn." He aimed the wand at Donnie and Harry. "You two. Turn back now or you're banned for life."

Harry began to twitch uncontrollably.

"Harry?" One of his companions patted the wolf's back. "Come on, mate. Everything's cool. Just shift back and we'll have another drink."

Another werewolf stepped in front of Donnie with his head lowered and made placating motions with his hands. "Donnie, come on. Let's call it a night, eh?"

The wolf's amber eyes fixated on his friend. For a fleeting moment, I thought everything was under control. Donnie sniffed the air between them and inched forward. The smaller guy's shoulders relaxed and his hands dropped to his side.

"Well done, Marco," someone called.

Donnie attacked.

He lunged at Marco, lifted him into the air like he weighed no more than a pint glass, and launched him across the room. Marco smashed into the window bearing the pub logo of the gold crown, red dragon, and white lion. Whimpering, he crashed to the ground.

The window cracked and splintered and a collective gasp followed. These windows had survived the Great Eruption and were irreplaceable. I didn't need to look at Simon's face to know he was devastated.

Shards of glass rained down on Marco and he rolled out of harm's way.

Donnie roared again like a beast staking his claim. In for a penny, in for a pound of flesh, apparently.

"Enough is enough," Simon bellowed.

His words were drowned out by an outburst of growls and snarls. It seemed that every werewolf in the pub was now agitated. My skin pricked at the sound. Fur was about to fly.

I cut a glance at the door. Kami and I could make it out, no problem. But I couldn't leave Simon to deal with this alone. The Crown was a safe space for the Knights of Boudica and if we didn't act now, we might lose it forever. Hell, the way these wolves were misbehaving, we might lose Simon.

Bones crunched and shreds of fabric dropped to the floor as wolves erupted from a dozen men. Two were manageable. Twelve hulking creatures were another story. Their jaws opened wide enough to swallow a pygmy goat whole. I thought of Herman back in my flat and shuddered. I really needed to not use my animal companions as measuring sticks for monster mouths.

Kami looked at me sideways. "Now what?"

At the very least we had to subdue them, but a dozen wolves with anger management issues would be no small feat.

I glanced at Simon, intending to get his approval. Magic was illegal without a license. Kami and I were licensed, but only in our capacity as knights, not as neighborhood vigilantes.

Simon's body started to shake with such force that he fell off the counter. The stun gun clattered to the floor and Kami rushed forward to grab it.

I was torn between dealing with the crazed wolves and helping Simon who was now seizing on the floor. What was happening? There was no way he'd turn in his own pub.

His bulging muscles and contorted face said otherwise.

Donnie lunged at me, making my decision for me.

"Stun Simon!" I shouted.

Kami didn't hesitate. She touched Simon with the end of the wand and zapped him.

I threw a punch at Donnie that had zero impact. The wolf's paw shot forward and whacked me in the solar plexus. The air left my lungs and I doubled over. Out of the corner of my eye, I saw Simon convulsing.

"Hey, the stun gun worked!" Kami yelled.

Dodging another blow from Donnie, I glanced over to see Simon back in human form. Unfortunately he was also unconscious.

Kami admired the stun gun. "We need one of these in the armory. Maybe even two."

Minka would never approve them. They were what she would consider 'superfluous.'

"You've still got a few furry friends to use it on," I called.

We needed to bar the door and keep the frenzied wolves from escaping into the night. They'd terrorize the city if they got out in their current condition.

I retrieved a dagger from my boot and raced to the door. Pricking my palm, I used a few drops of blood to create a simple ward. I wasn't excited by the prospect of being trapped in the pub right now, but there was no better option.

"Can you control any of them?" I asked Kami. Her primary magic was mind control, but it took a lot of effort and concentration. Weapons were her real specialty.

Kami focused. "Their minds are too...wild." She shook her head. "Their thoughts are frenetic, like a bunch of bucking stallions. There are too many anyway. I can't control a dozen minds at once."

A werewolf jumped forward and slashed across her front with a set of sharp claws.

"Hey!" she objected. "Minka would kill me if I ruined my uniform."

There were no marks on the uniform. One point for magical armor.

Donnie locked on me again and snarled.

Uh oh.

Too bad I couldn't influence a werewolf's mind. My ability to win over animals only extended to less complex brains. I'd have to stick to a good, old-fashioned beatdown.

I withdrew my axe from its sheath and used the blunt end to keep Donnie at bay. I had no interest in killing him or anyone else. I only wanted to prevent them from killing each other. From the puddles of blood on the floor, I wasn't convinced I'd succeed.

I cut a quick glance at Kami just as a werewolf lunged at her. Her head jerked sideways and she fell to the floor. The werewolf trampled her on his way to fight another opponent.

"Kami!"

She lay still on the floor. Six werewolves stood between us.

Magic zinged through me, responding to my torrent of emotions. If they killed Kami, I'd never forgive myself.

My skin began to vibrate. That was new.

Donnie snapped his jaws and narrowly missed my wrist. The vibration turned into a tugging sensation. Ignoring the discomfort, I jumped backward out of Donnie's reach.

Except somehow I was still there, fighting Donnie's massive muzzle.

What the...?

I looked at my hands and feet. No, I was definitely here and...another me was now fighting Donnie.

Magic pulsed through me again and my skin tugged. I was accustomed to my magic straining to be unleashed, but this sensation had a different quality to it. There was no silver glow involved, the telltale sign of my species. It was as though a magical layer was being peeled away like the skin of a potato, except I had no control over it. The magic was separating from me...*I* was somehow separating from me.

If I weren't so freaked out by the circumstances, I'd laugh at the idea of a myself as a magical potato.

Finally six versions of me fanned out in the pub and fought the werewolves that remained standing. A couple were unconscious like Simon.

Harry was dead.

I nearly tripped over him in an effort to take down Marco. I wasn't sure the wolf ever joined the fray. Whatever caused him to twitch uncontrollably seemed to have overtaken his body and killed him.

Terrific. Now the incident would have to be reported. Nobody loved bureaucracy as much as vampires—and Minka.

With a little air magic and a few well-placed kicks, multiple versions of me managed to subdue the rest of the wolves without killing anyone. Once the final wolf fell, my magical selves seemed to sense they were no longer needed and dissipated. Magic sparked in the air as the remnants faded away. The original me grabbed the stun gun still on the floor and ran around the room zapping wolves with it until they returned to human form. Like Simon, they were unconscious.

I was so shocked by my newfound ability that I could barely speak when Kami finally opened her eyes.

"What the hell happened?" Rubbing the back of her head, she pulled herself to a seated position. Her gaze swept the room where werewolf bodies lay scattered. "Holy hellfire. Is that your handiwork?"

"Sort of."

She lowered her voice. "Did you lose control of your magic?"

"Not in the way you think."

I didn't want to share what really happened. Not yet. I needed to do a little research first and understand it better. I'd always known I had untapped magical potential, but I usually kept a lid on it because of my fear of discovery. These magical versions of me...I had no control over their creation. I felt the way Harry looked when he examined his paws with confusion.

I pointed to Harry's body. "And just to be clear, I'm *not* responsible for him."

The werewolves stirred and one by one they regained consciousness.

Simon clambered to his feet. He surveyed the carnage and said, "Good grief."

Donnie was the first one at Harry's side. He checked for a pulse and pumped his friend's chest several times before being dragged off by two other wolves.

"We're so sorry, Simon," Marco said. "You know us. We're not like this."

"I'm sorry about Harry," Simon said.

I crossed the room to where the werewolves had clustered around their friend. "I hate to be the bearer of bad news, but we're duty-bound to report the death."

Donnie turned to me. "Not if you were never here."

"Even without knights in attendance, Simon is legally obligated to report it," I pointed out. "He could lose his liquor license if the authorities find out there was a cover-up."

An unspoken agreement seemed to pass between Donnie and Simon.

"We'll call the cleanup crew for Harry and then get out of your hair," Donnie said.

Simon nodded.

The large werewolf looked at me. "I know I fought you, but I'm fuzzy on the details. Whatever happened, I'm sorry."

"Me, too."

The werewolves huddled together in silence at the opposite end of the pub while Donnie placed a call.

"Kami and I will help you clean up."

"I don't know how you have the energy to do anything right now," Simon said. "How many wolves did you fight?"

"Enough." Simon didn't need to know my magic wasn't the kind that drained me. In fact, it was the exact opposite— the effort I used to contain my magic left me feeling drained. The more I used, the better I felt.

I picked up a large shard of glass and placed it in the pile that Kami and Simon had started.

"What do you think?" Kami whispered. "Turf war?"

If anyone were to get wind of unrest in a werewolf pack, it would be the one who served their ale. Although he was more of a lone wolf, Simon kept a finger on the pack pulse.

Simon shook his head. "They're in the same West End pack. Nice guys, too. They're usually a stable lot. This was..."

"A mess," Kami finished for him.

"A tragedy," I added.

Kami examined a piece of red glass before tossing it into the pile. "They were out of their minds," she said, never one to mince words.

Simon picked up the stun gun and placed the wand in his back pocket. "They're werewolves. It's how we fight."

Kami pressed her lips together. "You seem to forget who you're talking to. London and I have been in plenty of situations with wolves. Tonight was weird."

Simon observed the sorry state of the pub with a somber expression. His gaze flicked to the subdued group across the room. "It wasn't fun, I'll say that."

"You started to turn, too. The only reason you stopped is because Kami used your own weapon against you."

Simon patted the wand in his pocket. "Handy thing, isn't it?"

Kami pinned him with a hard stare. "You're avoiding the issue."

Simon lowered his gaze. "Yes, I started to shift. I don't know why. It wasn't deliberate. I think it was all that testosterone exploding in front of me. It affected me more than I realized."

I stared at the pile of broken glass. "I'm sorry about the window." As much as I tried not to get sentimental over objects, I couldn't help feeling a sense of loss.

Simon crouched beside the debris. "It might cost a mint, but maybe there's something a witch can do to salvage it. Free drinks for a month if you know anyone."

Kami coughed. "Only a month? This window is worth a year at least."

Simon grinned. "Willing to play hardball even at the worst of times, aren't you?"

Kami shrugged. "Hardball is the reason I've survived this long."

"Talk to Minka," I said. "She might know someone."

He nodded. "Good idea."

Kami inclined her head to Simon's weapon. "Where'd

you get that fancy wand anyway? I'd like to buy a couple for the armory."

His smile was a mixture of relief and satisfaction. "It was effective, wasn't it?"

"You know me. Always on the hunt for effective weapons."

"This was a lucky break," Simon admitted. "A patron and his friends had finished an entire cask of wine before they realized they didn't have enough to pay the bill. Gave me that instead. Said they're commonplace in Totnes where he's from."

I studied the wand. "Regional weapons. Who knew?"

Simon grabbed a nearby broom and started to sweep. "It paid for itself tonight."

"It saved your life." My gaze drifted across the room to where Harry's body remained. "Too bad we weren't able to use it on poor Harry in time."

"I've never seen anything like it," Kami said.

"Me neither." Simon leaned his chin on the broom handle and gazed at the fallen wolf. "And I hope I never do again."

3

I climbed to the fifth floor and unlocked the door to my flat. As usual it stuck to the frame and I leaned my weight against it. Multiple faces greeted me as I stumbled across the threshold.

"I'm home and it's been a tough day, so nobody better have peed on the carpet."

Such innocent expressions. You could've melted butter in their mouths. Except the cat, of course. Hera's face was the equivalent of *silence, witch-servant, and fetch me my catnip on a silver platter*.

There was, of course, a building rule that limited me to one animal companion which I blatantly ignored. It had been a minor issue because the former landlady was nosy and had a habit of entering my flat at inopportune moments. Now that she'd sacrificed herself for a lost cause, there was a new landlord to contend with, although this one seemed disinterested in nosing around his tenants' flats. His name was William and he had a habit of wandering the stairwell in a robe and slippers and muttering to himself.

Big Red was the first one to greet me. The red panda

curled his soft body around both my boots. He was only the size of a domestic cat, but his longer body allowed him the ability to trip both my feet at the same time.

I reached down to stroke his soft fur. "Hey, buddy. You miss me?"

Herman bleated. The pygmy goat was responsible for the majority of chewed items in the flat, which was one reason I didn't keep many material possessions. If Herman could angle his mouth around it, he'd be sure to taste test it.

"I bet you're all hungry. Let me feed you." I'd lost my appetite during the brawl at The Crown and had yet to recover it. Maybe after a shower and a good night's sleep.

Sandy darted ahead of me to the kitchen. Whereas Big Red wanted to be the first to greet me, the fennec fox wanted to be first at the food bowls. Priorities.

I retrieved a variety of food containers from the pantry and dished them out.

Jemima gently pecked my leg and I turned to address the Bantam hen. "Eat first. Then I'll change your diaper."

Without the diaper, the chicken would leave me unwanted gifts all over the flat. As far as I was concerned, the diaper was a small price to pay for not ending up at the market as someone's dinner.

As I returned the containers to the pantry, I glanced at the shelf where I stored baking ingredients. Dusted in white flour was the powerful elemental stone I'd acquired during my assignment for House Lewis. It was currently hidden here for safekeeping. I'd presented a fake stone to the king and queen who were unable to detect the difference. They already possessed the immortality stone. I refused to let the royal vampires have control over a powerful elemental stone, too.

The menagerie gobbled down their food like it was the

final meal of their lives and I opened the balcony to allow them fresh air. An impatient caw greeted me.

"Apologies, Barnaby. I didn't know you were here," I said to the raven. "You missed all the fun at the pub."

The raven fixed me with accusatory eyes, although I was pretty sure I was projecting.

"Harry's death was an accident," I said.

Barnaby cawed again and flew away. I tried not to take offense.

I'd mulled over the incident the whole way home. In light of the other wolves turning, I was confident Donnie and Harry would've shifted regardless of hitting the wall. The timing was simply an unfortunate coincidence.

At least that's what I kept telling myself. The appearance of magical mystery me gnawed at me. How did I manage to make multiple copies of myself? I knew there was magic I hadn't mastered, but this spectacular talent seemed like one I would've uncovered before now. It certainly didn't come from my father. Vampires didn't possess magic, and the one and only thing I knew about my father was his species. My mother didn't talk about him. She treated me the same way I treated my friends. The less I knew, the safer I'd be.

My mind was still buzzing when I crawled into bed an hour later. I closed my eyes and focused on happy memories. I tended to increase my chances of pleasant dreams when I chose a focal point in advance. My mother's image appeared in my mind's eye. I was eight years old and she was showing me how to manipulate fire. Every lesson was chosen carefully, prioritizing practicality and safety. Fire was versatile—it could keep me warm, help me see, and protect me. Sometimes I wondered what she'd think of me becoming a knight. Part of me thought she'd like that I dedicated my life to helping others. The other part of me worried she'd scold me for putting myself in danger every day when she'd worked so hard to hide me and keep me safe.

Thanks to my drifting mind, instead of pleasant dreams, I ended up with a montage of a vampire lineup where I was attempting to pick out my father while a clock ticked in the background. Not quite a nightmare but not exactly warm and fuzzy.

It was hard to imagine a vampire capable of sweeping my mother off her feet.

I rolled to the side and tucked my hands beneath my cheek in prayer form. I felt the warmth of Hera's body as the cat snuggled against my back and Big Red lay across my feet, pinning them to the mattress.

Knights tended to live somewhat solitary lives, but I was never lonely. There was always a whisker or a tail in my personal space. And they were good listeners, too. I credited them with keeping me sane.

My eyelids grew heavy and I was relieved to put the long day behind me. Finally I let go of the tension I'd been holding and welcomed sleep with open arms.

THE NEXT MORNING I arrived at the Knights of Boudica headquarters in Piccadilly Circus, feeling marginally better than the night before. There was no substitute for a good night's sleep. I sauntered into the Pavilion, pausing to greet Treena, the security guard. The building was originally constructed in the 1850s and was once the home of a music hall and a shopping arcade before succumbing to the effects of the Eternal Night and falling into disrepair. The original Knights of Boudica pooled their resources and bought the building for a song, then spent years fixing it up as their headquarters. As the only all-female banner, we went out of our way to keep a professional appearance. We didn't want to give anyone a reason to think less of us and that meant the best weapons we could afford, superior magical armor, and decent office space. Like our predecessors, we generally accepted the work nobody else wanted. We were the last port in a storm for the desperate, the poor, and the discreet —and people like Gerald Latham who apparently thought we'd do anything for a buck.

"Where's Trio?" I asked. I'd befriended the three-headed dog in a tunnel during an assignment and inadvertently ended up making her part of the team. It was either that or let her be killed. My flat was too cramped for a creature of her size so now she lived here as a watchdog.

"Briar took her for a walk. Two of her heads were whining," Treena said. "I heard The Crown blew up. Know anything about that?"

I held up my hand as though swearing an oath. "I know absolutely nothing about The Crown blowing up."

Treena eyed me suspiciously but didn't ask any follow-up questions.

I was halfway to my desk when Minka pounced on me. "I heard there was an incident at The Crown last night. It's closed for renovations."

"Is it?" I maintained a neutral expression. Although she was a witch, Minka Tarlock served mostly in an administrative role. Her specialty was spells, which weren't as handy in the field as other types of magic. When you were in the midst of a knock-down, drag-out fight with a minotaur, you didn't have time to light candles and mix potions.

"You were there. I heard all about it from Simon." Minka regarded me as she pulled her dark hair into a sleek ponytail. If she talked less, you might notice the bronze skin and wide-set brown eyes inherited from her Asian father and the willowy frame and straight nose passed down from her Nordic mother.

Her mouth was always moving, however, and she left you no choice but to focus on the barrage of questions and comments being hurled at you. More than once Kami remarked that the armory needed a shield for the sole purpose of deflecting conversations with Minka.

"I heard you were drunk and wrecked the place and it's going to cost a small fortune to fix."

I sincerely doubted she'd heard any of that from Simon. He wanted to keep the actual events quiet and had no reason to capitulate to Minka's demands for information.

I smiled. "Then I suppose there's nothing I can tell you that you don't already know."

She pursed her lips together and thrust out a sheet of paper. "I expect a full report on last night's adventure."

I ignored the paper and kept walking. "Kami said she would do it." Technically Gerald Latham wasn't my client, so the report had to be completed by Kami unless she was incapacitated.

Kami ambled in behind me. "What did I say I'd do?"

Minka waved the same sheet of paper at her. "Report on the Latham case. Did you successfully complete it?"

"Yep." Kami snatched the paper from Minka's hand and kept walking.

"London told us what happened at The Crown," Minka said.

My jaw unhinged. "Seriously? I'm right here, Minka."

"Nice try." Kami slid behind her desk and rested her boots on the edge. "I don't know anything about what happened there and neither does London."

A monstrous creature loped into view. Briar unhooked Trio's leash and patted the middle head. "Such a good girl."

Three tongues dropped to the sides of their respective mouths.

"Does she really need to be on a leash?" I asked.

"Yes." Briar hung the leash on a hook on the wall. "We don't all have your wrangling skills and I don't want to be responsible for anything happening to her."

Briar Niall had a heart of gold and who was I to challenge it? I'd say it was because, as a shapeshifter with the ability to morph into monstrous creatures, she felt a kinship with the dog—except Briar's tenderness extended to children and inanimate objects. She still slept with the same teddy bear she'd snuggled since infancy. I feared the day that teddy bear lost its stuffing. Briar would lose her mind.

"The dog's eating too much," Minka complained. "She needs to be put on a diet."

"Don't body shame her," Briar objected.

I cast a critical eye at the dog. "She looks the same to me. A bit meatier, but considering she was half starved when I met her, that's a good thing."

Ione Sheehan hurried into the open-plan office, her cheeks flushed. "The next time a client hires us to remove a troublesome flock of magpies, please give the job to someone else."

Kami smirked. "Why? What happened?"

Ione flopped into her chair. "You don't want to know."

"Actually I do." Kami swung her feet to the floor and leaned forward intently. "I had a rough night, Ione. Throw me a bone."

"Fine." Ione leaned her elbows on the desk and rubbed her face. "Mrs. Alden asked us to take care of her bird problem, which turned out to be the wrong number of magpies making an appearance on her fence."

"The wrong number?" Briar queried. "You mean she's missing one?"

Ione shook her head. "You know the old nursery rhyme—one for sorrow, two for mirth, three for a funeral, four for a birth."

Minka frowned. "I thought it was two for joy and then five for heaven, six for hell, seven for the devil, his own self."

Ione sighed. "According to Mrs. Alden, there are typically an even number of magpies on her fence, but last week they were only showing up in odd numbers."

I bit back a smile. "And an odd number of magpies is bad?"

"Very bad," Ione confirmed. Tall and slender with light brown hair tied in a knot at the base of her neck, the earth witch looked more like someone ready to lead a classroom of children in song than a knight ready to take down a monster with a bow and arrow.

"Especially one single magpie," Minka chimed in.

"She insisted one of her neighbors was trying to curse her and asked me to find out which one to put a stop to it," Ione continued.

Kami slotted her fingers together and cradled the back of her head. "So? Was she right?"

Ione opened a canteen of water and drank greedily. Then she wiped her mouth and said, "She was, as a matter of fact."

Kami's mouth formed a small 'o'. "Plot twist! I thought for sure it was just going to be due to magpie migration."

Ione took another swig from the canteen. "I found a cage full of magpies in her neighbor's shed. Apparently every time more than one appeared on the fence, the neighbor would snatch it and lock it in the cage so there'd only be one."

"One for sorrow." Kami whistled. "Did the neighbor say why?"

"He said Mrs. Alden had stolen his curry recipe and claimed it as her own during the neighborhood curry competition. She won first prize. When he confronted her, she denied it."

Kami choked back laughter. "And this was his revenge? Combat by magpie?"

"It seemed to work," Ione said, shrugging. "She was upset enough to hire me."

"Please tell me you set those poor magpies free." Briar leaned down and rubbed Trio's exposed belly. The monstrous dog looked ridiculous with her legs splayed and her three heads bobbing.

"Of course. And I told Mrs. Alden the truth." Ione stared vacantly at the wall. "Great goddess. I really hope our new neighbors are nice."

Briar perked up. "New neighbors?"

"Neera and I are moving into our new flat this week, remember? Once we've got furniture for you to sit on, we'll have everyone over for a party."

"Where is it again?" If she mentioned it before, I'd forgotten. It would be nice to have knights who lived closer to me. We seemed to be scattered throughout the city, which was one reason we met up at The Crown after work. Location, location, location.

"Near Paddington," Ione said. "I wouldn't have minded staying in our same flat, but ever since the tribute center opened at the end of the block, the street's been teeming with vampires." She shuddered. "When we realized the lease was coming to an end, we decided to take the leap."

As vampires' low-hanging fruit, humans were required to register as blood donors for their local tribute center. Like jury duty, it was set up as a lottery system, except not all donors survived the ordeal. Supernaturals were exempt. Vampires had better uses for magic users, like keeping plants alive and protecting the territory from invaders.

"The centers should all be on the outskirts of the city," Minka said.

Kami batted her eyelashes in a mock innocent fashion. "But then how can our vampire overlords remind us they're in charge? Part of the intimidation factor is having the centers smack in the middle of every bustling neighborhood." She delivered the Latham report to my desk for me to co-sign.

Ione squirmed. "When you see them all standing in the queue...It makes me queasy."

I scanned the report, signed it, and handed it back to Kami. "Tribute centers are better than the alternative." Before the tribute centers were established, vampires were free to feed on anybody they encountered. People lived in constant fear.

"Did your boyfriend tell you that?" Kami asked. "Speaking of the Demon of House Duncan, has he invited you to participate in any Britannia Day events tomorrow?"

I narrowed my eyes at her.

Minka straightened in her chair, adopting the tone of a lecturer. "I highly doubt Prince Callan would participate in festivities that celebrated his handover to House Lewis. If it weren't for Queen Britannia, he'd still be in Scotland with his family instead of a hostage to House Lewis."

"Not necessarily," Kami argued. "If House Duncan had won the Battle of Britannia, Callan still might've ended up here, just as the future king instead of a hostage." She dropped the completed report on Minka's desk and winked. "Don't say I never gave you anything."

Minka glowered in return. "Don't you have somewhere you need to be?"

"She does, in fact," a familiar voice said.

Multiple heads swiveled to the entrance where Simon stood. He twisted a hat in his hands.

"Hey, Simon," I said. "How are you holding up?"

His gaze met mine. "I need you and Kami."

A lump formed in my throat. "The authorities?"

"Just the pack," he said. "I tried to keep you out of it, I swear, but they'd gotten a full account from at least two of the werewolves present. Now there's an internal inquiry."

"And if we refuse?" I asked.

Simon's expression clouded over. "I wouldn't recommend it. If you don't come willingly, they have a backup plan."

Minka folded her arms. "That backup plan better not involve busting into the Pavilion. Tell them we have an attack hellhound."

Trio seemed to sense she was the topic of conversation and tilted her three heads upside down to look at Simon.

Kami rolled her eyes. "Yes, one look at Trio and they'll be running out of here with their tails between their legs."

"We'll come with you," I said. If nothing else, we owed it to Simon.

Kami reached for the dagger on her desk. "We can bring weapons, right?"

"You can bring them. Not sure you'll get to keep hold of them, though."

Kami withdrew her hand. "Fine. I'll bring a cheap one." She opened the drawer of her desk and rooted around for the inexpensive blade. "Here it is."

Minka squinted. "Hey, that's the one I bought you last year for your birthday."

Kami quickly hid the dagger behind her back. "I'm sure it isn't. I keep that one in a special place." She turned and grimaced at us before hurrying to join Simon and I at the exit. "If we're not back in two hours, call the cavalry."

Briar glanced up from her desk, frowning. "We *are* the cavalry."

"Right," Kami pivoted to me. "We can handle a room full of werewolves, can't we?"

I remembered the magical versions of me that fought the crazed wolves in The Crown.

"I'd bet my life on it."

4

The West End Werewolf Pack held their meetings in a building on Sloane Street that once housed a department store called Harvey Nichols. I quite liked the idea of a tribunal set up in a former lingerie department. Added a touch of class to the event.

We arrived at security and were immediately whisked away to the second floor. Simon was summoned first. Kami and I were asked to wait in a separate room and were offered water and homemade shortbread, which we declined.

"Are you sure? Susan makes a mean shortbread. It's the envy of every household in the West End." The werewolf removed the lid from the tin and showed off the golden biscuits.

Kami nudged me. "Go on, London. We don't want to be rude."

Kami had a weakness for biscuits. Mine was chocolate.

"You don't happen to have any dipped in chocolate, do you?" Kami asked, anticipating my desire.

The werewolf's lips curled into a half smile, half snarl.

"If we did, they'd be gone by now. I can count the number of wolves on one hand that don't like chocolate in this pack."

I'd wolfed down two biscuits—pun intended—when another werewolf appeared in the doorway. "London Hayes."

I wiped the crumbs from my lips and raised my hand. "That's me."

He crooked a finger. "You're up."

"Where's Simon?" I asked.

"He was escorted out once they finished questioning him," the werewolf said.

"I want to wait here for Kami when I'm finished," I told him. "I'm not leaving her behind."

Kami shoved another biscuit in her mouth. I had a feeling she'd make herself sick if I took too long. I resolved to talk fast.

The werewolf opened a set of double doors and stepped aside. "Have fun," he whispered and closed the doors behind me. The sound echoed in the cavernous room.

I stared straight ahead at a long table. Three werewolves were seated facing the rest of the room. Two smaller tables lined the first row, followed by benches. The room was packed with werewolves. I didn't think I'd ever been in close proximity to so many at once.

"Come forward and state your name," the middle werewolf said. She gestured to the empty chair at the table to my left. Hers was the shorter of three heads and her brown hair was styled in a no-nonsense blunt cut. The lines on her face suggested mid-to-late fifties and the three-inch scar on her cheek suggested a hard-won existence.

"London Hayes, Knight of Boudica."

"Welcome, Miss Hayes. We appreciate your cooperation in this matter. My name is Nicolette Dumont. The other members of the tribunal are Jervis Tinicum and Romeo Rice."

Jervis was surprisingly thin for a werewolf. His face was mostly covered by a thick beard and mustache, and his copper head was bald except for a one-inch line of hair. He looked like a broomstick with missing bristles.

"We understand you were at The Crown last night. Is that correct?" Jervis asked.

"Yes."

"And you witnessed Donald Simmons transform?" Jervis asked.

"That is correct."

"And Harry Burns?" he added.

"Yes. If you're going to name them all, I'll save you the trouble because I don't know their names. Every single werewolf in the pub shifted."

Out of the corner of my eye, I noticed Romeo hide a smirk behind his hand. He was the largest of the three with thick, dark hair that covered his head and I had no doubt also covered his chest—and quite possibly his back.

"In your estimation, were the transformations unprovoked?" Nicolette asked.

I faltered. "I couldn't say. The group became progressively louder and more unruly as the evening went on."

Nicolette peered at me intently. "Any idea why?"

I shrugged. "Too much ale?"

"You couldn't hear the content of their discussion?" Romeo asked. He was attractive in that burly, lumberjack way. He also slouched, which I appreciated. Made the whole affair feel slightly less formal.

"No. I was focused on my own conversation at the time. We just heard the volume steadily increase until Simon was warning them not to shift."

"Ah, yes. Your conversation with your companion." Nicolette scanned the sheet of paper in front of her. "Kamikaze Marwin. Interesting names, the two of you. Do they reassign you names when you join the banner?"

"No. Those are our given names."

Romeo grinned. "I have no room to talk."

"Your mother loved literature, clearly," Nicolette said. She shifted her attention back to me. "And I suppose your mother loved geography."

"History, actually, but I suppose they're related subjects."

Jervis squirmed in his seat. He seemed anxious to move forward with the proceedings. "According to our report, you inserted yourself into a volatile situation. Why?"

"I tried to diffuse the situation."

"By hanging from a light fixture and kicking Donnie in the chest?" Romeo asked. His mouth twitched, seemingly amused.

"He was holding Harry over his head, ready to dwarf-toss him. I only intended to subdue him." I pinned them with a hard look. "I was under the impression you needed information. If I'd known you intended to put me on trial, I would've brought a barrister with me."

Romeo snorted. "Fair enough."

"Tell us what you witnessed with regard to Harry Burns," Nicolette said.

"He seemed to shift against his will. Same with Simon. Simon's in the middle of brawls all the time and never once shifted. He knows how to control himself." I heard murmurs of assent behind me. "Harry seemed to suffer some kind of seizure. His body twitched in his wolf form and he...died."

"No one assaulted him?" Jervis asked.

"It's hard to say. Fur and fists were flying, but I didn't see anyone attack Harry specifically. In fact, I'm pretty sure he was the first one on the floor when everyone started fighting. If anything, he should've been safer there."

They consulted each other in silence.

"The participating wolves have a hazy recollection of events," Nicolette said. "One claimed there were at least six knights fighting them, whereas others identified only two."

"Kami and I were the only knights present; that is correct." I made sure to maintain a neutral expression. Let them believe the wolves were too dazed and confused to remember properly.

Nicolette steepled her fingers together and regarded me. "Would you blame anyone for last night's tragic event? You may speak freely."

I was tempted to make a joke about whoever supplied the ale, but an image of Harry's lifeless face pierced my memories and I shook my head instead.

"No, ma'am. As far as I can tell, it was a tragic accident."

Romeo leaned forward. "And we understand that you and Miss Marwin agreed not to report the death to the authorities."

"We did for Simon's sake."

"We hope you will continue to honor that agreement," Romeo said.

"That's the plan."

"Thank you, Miss Hayes. You are dismissed." Nicolette motioned toward the double doors.

I walked past the rows of curious werewolves. It seemed like every set of eyes followed me as I exited the room. The double doors closed behind me with an echoing clink.

"That didn't take long," Kami said, once the werewolf escorted me back to the waiting room.

"I was concise."

"Shocker."

The werewolf smiled at Kami. "Your turn, beautiful."

"Hey," I objected. "I didn't get any compliments."

The female werewolf held up the tin of shortbread. "Another biscuit?"

"Distracting me with food? It's like you know me." I reached into the tin.

Kami's interview took only slightly less time than mine. We made it to the first floor when we were intercepted by the lumberjack from the tribunal.

Romeo approached us with an easy swagger. "Could I have a word with you in private?"

Kami and I traded looks.

"You, Miss Hayes."

"Don't mind me," Kami interjected. "I'll just stand awkwardly at the opposite end of the vestibule."

"No need," Romeo said. "We can go to my office." He pointed. "It's on this floor, just across the way."

"I'll wait right here," Kami said.

Romeo guided me to his office. With its dark wood furniture and musky smell, the room emanated rugged masculinity.

He loomed over me, a good foot taller. I hadn't realized just how tall he was until now. His teeth were whiter than I would've expected. Vampires used special fluid to keep bloodstains off their teeth so I was accustomed to their blinding smiles. Werewolves weren't usually as fastidious.

"You're distracted," he said. "It's my teeth, isn't it?"

I was taken aback by the accuracy of his guess. "How did you know?"

He appeared crushed. "Jervis made fun of me earlier. I tried a new product and I guess it works a little too well."

I couldn't help but laugh. "Depends on your goal, I guess."

He leaned a muscular forearm on the wall over my head. "What if my goal is to attract beautiful women? Is it working?"

"Please don't tell me you brought me into your office to hit on me."

"Would that be so horrible?"

I folded my arms and looked up at him. "I'm on a schedule, Mr. Rice. What is it you wanted to say to me?"

"Romeo."

"I'm on a schedule, Romeo. I only came here as a favor to Simon."

"The Crown owner is a friend of yours?"

"Friend might be a stretch, but I'm a frequent patron at his pub."

He glanced at the closed door. "And Kamikaze Marwin? Is she a friend or are you two romantically involved?"

"Does it matter?"

"Not really. I was only curious." He removed his arm and a professional mask dropped into place. "I'd like to hire you."

I blinked. "Why?"

He motioned to the chair opposite his desk. "Have a seat and I'll tell you."

"If you called me in here to discuss a job, why not include Kami?"

"Because I'm trying to keep this quiet and you impressed me during the tribunal."

"If you hire me, I have to complete paperwork at the office." That wasn't strictly true, of course, but given that I'd recently tried to hide a job for House Lewis from my banner, I wasn't sure a repeat performance was such a smart idea. I already kept enough secrets from the other knights.

His gaze felt like a weight pressing against my chest. "What if I consider this a matter of national security?"

"Then you should probably contact someone at House Lewis."

He grunted. "Over my dead body." His dark eyes glinted. "What if the pack offers to foot the bill to repair The Crown?"

"You can do that?"

"Simon isn't a paid member of the pack, so we have discretion whether to assist him. I can make certain that we do in exchange for your cooperation."

"Don't you think you should offer to foot the bill anyway? If it weren't for twelve of your pack members turning, the pub would be fine."

"Seems to me they were overserved."

"I told you he's not a friend. What makes you think your offer would persuade me?"

He fiddled with his pen. "You strike me as a creature of habit, London. May I call you London? The Crown is somewhere you frequent because you feel safe there. Secure."

"I didn't feel very safe and secure when your friends went nuts."

His face hardened. "That's the reason I've asked you here. Before I tell you more, I need to know—are you in or out?"

I thought of poor Simon and the damage to The Crown. "In."

Romeo wore a satisfied smile. "Do you know what a berserker is?"

"Wolves who lose control and go on a rampage."

"Close enough. Sounds like what happened at The Crown, doesn't it?"

My hands squeezed the arms of the chair. "You think they're berserkers?"

"Based on what we know about the condition, yes. I was part of the cleanup crew that showed up after you left." His expression clouded over. "I heard enough to convince me."

The news floored me. Berserker wolves in Britannia City was a nightmare scenario.

"But they're members of your pack." If they had berserkers among them, I would know. The whole city would know.

"Yes, and they've never shown signs before. This has shocked us all, which is why I'd like you to investigate for us. You'll be compensated. The Crown is only meant to be an extra incentive because of the risk involved."

"Is this your first experience with berserkers in your pack?"

"I've never known one to cross into our territory, no, which is why I'd like you to go to Devon."

"Devon. Why start there?"

"Because that's where the berserkers are. There's a man I'd like you to see who might be able to provide information."

"Why not go yourself?"

He spread his arms wide. "Because I have ample work that keeps me in the city."

"And because you don't want to go." I peered at him. "The countryside makes you nervous."

His expression grew thoughtful. "For as long as I can remember, there were rumors about wolves in the Southwest. Some believe they're a different species of wolf because their behavior is so erratic. So different from ours. Unable to shift at will. They transform in a fit of rage and then can't shift back without help. Or they want to shift and can't. It's as if they lose autonomy over their own bodies."

"Do you think there's a berserker bloodline?"

"Some believe there's a genetic defect passed down from generation to generation. It makes sense they'd be concentrated within a certain geographic location. Those wolves would grow up and procreate with each other."

"What do you believe?"

"Up until last night, I had no reason to question it, but now..." He exhaled. The breath seemed designed to stop whatever he was about to say rather than an emotional release.

I leaned forward. "Romeo, if you want my help, I need to know everything you know."

He opened the top drawer of his desk and produced a bottle of antacid tablets. "You see what this is doing to me?" He unscrewed the lid and popped a tablet into his mouth. "As far as we know, the berserkers are concentrated in areas south and east of Exeter. A few months ago, a nasty storm blew through the region and wreaked havoc on one of the country estates. Albemarle. Knocked down a wall that was already weak and crumbling. Locals went to help restore the wall at least partially, to keep the house from being vulnerable to the elements. Some went to steal whatever supplies they could carry."

The news didn't surprise me. It happened here when the churches were destroyed by Queen Britannia. Residents crawled out of the woodwork to take bricks, stones—anything they might be able to use.

"What does this have to do with the wolves?"

He licked his lips. "At some point between the storm and the start of repairs, the berserkers ceased to exist."

"They disappeared?"

"No. Those same wolves suddenly had control over their transformations. They became just like the rest of us."

A light flickered in my mind. "But now there seem to be berserker wolves outside Devon where they haven't been before."

He pointed a delighted finger at me. "Now you're getting it."

"So you think there was something in the rubble of the country house that turns normal wolves into berserkers and now that something has found its way to Britannia City?"

"That's the theory I'd like you to investigate."

Wow. What a whopper of a bombshell. "If this object causes werewolves to go berserk and it's no longer in the countryside, why are you concerned about going?"

He dumped a second tablet into his hand and tossed it into his mouth. "What makes us believe there's only one of these objects that makes us nuts? I don't want to risk going down there to investigate and losing control."

"But if the object is here now, you're susceptible to it. The danger is even greater if you stay."

He crunched the tablet. "I was at the pub afterward and nothing happened to me. Go to Albemarle and speak to Lord Bowman. Find out whatever you can and report back to me but be discreet. I want to keep this limited to you and me. No need to frighten the pack."

"I'll need special dispensation to enter House Peyton territory." And if I couldn't reveal the purpose of the journey, that made crossing the border even trickier.

He tapped the pads of his thumbs together. "And here I pegged you for a resourceful knight."

"Are you sure you don't want to hire someone already in Devon? Might be easier."

"I haven't met any knights in Devon, London, but I have

met you." He gave me a long look. "And from what I've seen and heard, I think you're the right person for the job. I want you to find out exactly what's causing this so we can control it before it controls us."

I started to view his offer as an opportunity. I'd never been to Devon, although I'd picked up details here and there from my mother. Seaside towns. Castles and country houses. Dramatic landscapes. Despite the fight for power between House Lewis and House Duncan, much of Devon and Cornwall remained unspoiled because House Peyton managed to stay out of the fray. The royal vampires there hadn't bowed to pressure from Queen Britannia or the Highland King, wisely opting not to choose a side.

"I'll have to do a bit of research before I go."

"Whatever gets the job done." He made a noise at the back of his throat. "One more thing."

"Yes?"

"How about dinner upon your return? I know an incredible steak restaurant. It costs the earth, but once you taste the meat in your mouth, you'll feel it's worth it."

Their meat or his? "Thanks, but I'm not interested." In either option.

"How about an intimate dinner at my penthouse then? I can promise you a gorgeous view of the city." He opened his arms. "Or I'm open to other options that include satiating an appetite."

"First, I'm a vegetarian. Second, I'm a Knight of Boudica and it's important that I maintain a certain level of professionalism."

"Fair enough. It was worth a try. It isn't every day I cross paths with a beautiful woman who can drop-kick a pub full of unruly werewolves." His thick eyebrows lifted. "Very sexy, by the way."

I rose to my feet, effectively ending the meeting. "I'll update you when I get back."

I left the office in a hurry and ushered Kami out of the building before she could start peppering me with questions. She managed to make it all the way across the street before the questions spilled out one after the other. She barely left space for answers in her hurry to ask them all at once.

"You're worse than Minka right now." I chose to answer the only one I could. "Yes, he asked to take me to dinner. I turned him down."

"Why would you do that? When someone offers to buy you a meal, the answer is always yes."

I shot her an annoyed look. "It absolutely isn't. I can feed myself, thank you very much."

She glanced over her shoulder as though she could see him standing behind us. "He was hot if you like the burly werewolf type."

"Which I don't."

Kami smiled. "Because you prefer the royal vampire type."

I winced. "Don't be ridiculous."

"I wish Romeo had asked me. I'd be more than happy to be his Juliet."

"Then you'd both end up dead."

Kami scrunched her nose. "Is that how it ends? I thought they got married."

"It's a tragedy. They only get married at the end in the comedies."

She snapped her fingers in dismay.

"Anyway, if he knew you better, I have no doubt he would've asked you instead. He seems to have me confused with someone far more appealing."

Kami patted her concealed dagger. "Ah, well. His loss. I have my special companion right here."

"And I have a half dozen special companions waiting for me at my flat. I don't need Romeo or anyone else."

Kami shook her head. "You and those animals. No wonder there's no room for a man. He wouldn't even have a spot to sit on the sofa."

"There's plenty of room as long as I don't sit there, too."

Kami stopped when we reached the corner. "I need to head back to my flat."

"Now?" It wasn't even five o'clock. It seemed early for Kami to ditch work.

She mumbled something unintelligible.

I cupped a hand next to my ear. "What was that?"

"I have to get changed."

My eyes widened. "You can't be serious. All this talk about Romeo and you already have a date? How do you keep managing to meet men?"

"You meet them, too. You just don't show any interest in them." She jabbed a thumb over her shoulder in the direction of pack headquarters. "Case in point."

"Who is this guy?"

"Not to worry, boss. He's been fully vetted."

I folded my arms. "You sure about that? Because the last time you went out with someone, you thought he was handy with a sword and it turned out to be a butter knife."

Kami's cheeks turned pink. "This one is a repairman."

"What does he repair?"

She lifted her chin and a note of pride slipped into her voice. "Anything, really. Refrigerator. Hoover. He's multi-talented."

My mouth dropped open. "I can't believe it. This is a second date!"

She lowered her eyes to the pavement. "Third, technically."

I punched her arm. "Kamikaze Marwin, you've been holding out on me."

"Can you blame me? I was mortified after the last time. I want to wait and see whether this one's a keeper before I mention anything."

"Sounds like he might be."

"I was going to decide after tonight. He's taking me for sushi."

I tapped my foot. "Name?"

"Charles."

"Not Charlie or Chuck?"

She shook her head. "He prefers Charles."

"Human?"

"Yeah." She hugged herself, rubbing her arms in the process. "I wish he wasn't, but you can't help what someone is."

We agreed on that score. "Presumably he makes a living."

Her head bobbed enthusiastically. "Definitely. Nobody wants to get rid of their machines. Too hard to replace. His work is in high demand."

Made sense. "When do I get to meet him?"

She smiled. "I'll let you know tomorrow. Deal?"

"Deal."

Kami and I parted ways at the intersection. I couldn't be angry with her for holding out on me when I was keeping secrets of my own. As much as I hated to lie to my best friend, protecting her was more important than confiding in her. After all, a deceived friend was preferable to a dead one.

5

Britannia Day meant a parade through the city and more vampires than I cared to count. My best course of action was to keep to my section of the city today and avoid the crowds. Actually my best course of action was to stay home until tomorrow, but that wasn't an option when I had work to do.

The library was only a short stroll from my flat, which made it a convenient place to seek refuge, as well as information on berserkers in Devon. It was open every day of the year, holiday or not.

I entered the building and inhaled the scent of leather-bound books. I felt as comfortable among the stacks of books as I did in the armory among the weapons. It helped that I was a known entity to the three head librarians. Pedro Gutierrez was the one most willing to assist me. According to him, Adelaide and Garrison were wary of me. When Adelaide saw me approach, she had a tendency to duck behind the counter. That was probably because of the time I presented her with the head of an amorak and asked her to identify its country of origin. In my defense, I didn't have my camera with me to take a photo and I offered to clean and disinfect the counter afterward. I could be considerate when it suited me.

"Good morning, Pedro."

The librarian glanced up from the book on the counter. "Miss Hayes. I do hope you're here with more research questions. I haven't had any as interesting as your last inquiries."

Pedro had been instrumental in helping me uncover information in my search for Princess Davina. I hadn't shared the details of that assignment with him, but it wasn't the thrill of the chase that energized him, it was the acquisition of knowledge he didn't previously possess.

"You're in luck. I have a new client and I need to see everything you have on the subject of berserker werewolves and an estate called Albemarle in Devon."

His face registered a combination of surprise and curiosity. "Fascinating. I know we have a selection of books on aberrant species. If you'll follow me."

He came out from behind the counter and guided me to a Reading Room where he directed me to an empty desk away from the other patrons. He knew I liked my space.

"Make yourself at home and I'll be back in a jiffy." He motioned to a stack of books on a table behind me. "There are resources out in honor of Britannia Day if you care to peruse them while I locate your books."

"Thank you."

I leafed through the historical accounts of the Battle of Britannia while Pedro went in search of my requests. Queen Britannia had been the most formidable vampire in recorded history and it still seemed incredible that she was dead. Paranoid and ruthless, it was she who decided the dhampir were a threat to the future of vampires and demanded our execution.

Her goal was to maintain pure vampire bloodlines, so she discouraged relationships between vampires and other species through tax credits and other means. Human-vampire unions were particularly distasteful to her because she viewed one species as superior to the other. If it had been solely up to Britannia, humans would have been sent to slaughterhouses as food for vampires. According to insider accounts, it was King Casek who convinced her that tribute centers were preferable to slaughterhouses from a public relations standpoint as well as the fact that human blood tasted better when it was uncoerced. I had no idea whether the latter was true since I'd never tasted it. Although I was half vampire, I didn't inherit the need or desire for human blood.

I paged through book after book, scanning the entries about the events of this day twenty years ago. The writeup of the battle's tragic events were exactly the same in every book. The queen's sacrifice turned the tide of the battle and allowed House Lewis to successfully defend the territory against House Duncan's attack. The ferocious vampire queen who cared nothing for humans died the most noble of deaths—in defense of her subjects.

It reeked of propaganda.

By the time Pedro returned with his arms laden with books, my head was swimming with thoughts about Queen Britannia's untimely death. I swept the books aside so he could set the new ones in front of me.

"What do you know about Queen Britannia?"

As usual Pedro seemed thrilled by a request for information. "We have an entire wing devoted to her apart from the books currently on display for Britannia Day. Are you looking for specific information?"

"Not really." I fell silent, uncertain what I wanted to

know. "Have you ever wondered about the Battle of Britannia?"

He frowned. "Wondered what?"

"No one seems to question the sketchy details of her death. There were no eyewitnesses, only an announcement. She was the most feared vampire in the realm. She died during the decisive battle and House Lewis won despite her death. Why didn't the other Houses charge in when they heard the news of her death to take advantage of the power vacuum? Why didn't House Duncan take advantage of the turn of events?"

Maybe it was because House Lewis retained possession of the immortality stone. It was the stone from which all vampires were said to have been granted the power of immortality. The general population didn't know of its existence, of course, but I did. I couldn't underestimate its importance.

"The Highland King was gravely wounded during the battle, don't forget. They weren't sure whether he'd survive. He was hardly in a position to take advantage of the queen's death."

"What about Prince Callan?"

"He was still many miles away."

"Birmingham," I said softly. Everybody knew what happened in Birmingham. The city never recovered from the wrath of the young vampire. Although I'd never been there, I'd heard accounts of the toll his brief stop took on the city and its people. It also upset the residents that House Lewis didn't make an effort to aid their recovery afterward. They felt abandoned by their king and queen, but there was nothing to do except clean up and carry on.

"Most travelers moving north and south circumvent Birmingham," Pedro continued. "I haven't been that way myself, but I've heard it's a wasteland. Most respectable vampires have abandoned it for more hospitable cities."

"Who controls it now?"

Pedro wore a thoughtful expression. "Obviously it's under the official control of House Lewis, but once the vampires left, shifters felt comfortable moving in. They tend to be the species that fills a vacuum left by vampires."

It made sense. Many witches and wizards enjoyed a decent standard of living thanks to vampires, but shifters didn't share in that wealth. Packs weren't willing to band together against vampires either. They were oftentimes too busy fighting amongst themselves for control.

Pedro shuddered. "What twelve-year-old has the power and brutality required to destroy an entire city? It was wise of House Lewis to take the boy as a hostage. I can only imagine what he'd be capable of now if he'd remained in his father's care."

An image of the deadly but handsome vampire flashed in my mind. "If he was such a threat, why didn't they kill him?"

Pedro blinked at me. "Because that's not how treaties work. If House Lewis had murdered the boy, there would've been an all-out war. The other Houses would've waded into the fray. At that point, the other Houses were willing to let Duncan and Lewis expend their resources and beat themselves silly. It was a tactical move."

Yes, that was the same thought I'd had earlier about House Peyton. They'd stood back and waited to see where the chips fell.

"Don't you think it's strange that King Casek has never been a part of Britannia Day?"

According to reports, the celebration began at the

request of a young Prince Maeron to honor his mother's sacrifice.

"I imagine the king's heartbreak prevents him from joining the festivities. It must be a terrible reminder of his loss."

I stared at the book in front of me. "I suppose." It was time to shift gears and conduct the research I was actually being paid to do.

"Is there anything else I can get for you, miss?" Pedro asked.

I tapped the book on the top of the pile. "I think I'm good for now, thank you."

I dove right in. I'd always been a fast reader, a skill that served me well as a child when I wanted to finish every book on my nightstand before bedtime. My mother would have to pry books out of my hands and force me to go to sleep. Sighing deeply, I leaned an elbow on the desk. I'd give anything for those pointless arguments now.

I flipped through the indices of the books hunting for keywords like berserker and Albemarle. Although there were references to the earl and the history of the estate, there was nothing specific to the house's construction. There was only slightly more information on berserkers. Of course, it was difficult to obtain information on a species you couldn't get close enough to study without risking life and limb—assuming that berserkers were a different species.

What if we were wrong?

It seemed like the kind of thing we'd know by now. Then again, every day seemed to herald the discovery of a new species of fish or insect. And who could forget the monsters that arrived with the Great Eruption. If people could be mistaken about the existence of supernaturals, why not be wrong about the origin of berserkers?

After only a couple hours, I'd exhausted the available references. I learned a few facts I didn't know, but nothing that shed light on Romeo's questions. I'd have to rely on my visit to Devon for that.

Pedro seemed to take it as a personal failure that I didn't find exactly what I was looking for. I assured him that I hadn't expected to and it was only knowledge for knowledge's sake. A lie, but one I knew would satisfy him.

As I exited the library, I checked my phone for messages. Two voicemails. Because of the atmospheric changes, satellites were unreliable, which meant phones didn't always work properly.

I listened to the first voicemail from Minka who was conducting inventory and wanted to know whether I had the new crossbow. No one had checked it out but it was missing. It didn't take a detective to figure out which one of us had the crossbow.

I skipped to the next voicemail. Stevie asked me to call her straight away, so I did.

"Hey, Stevie."

"How busy are you on a scale of examining your cuticles to saving the world?"

"Somewhere in between?"

"Perfect. I need your help. I've got a lead on a thief I've been tracking and I'd love some company."

Inwardly I groaned. "It's Britannia Day. The last thing I want to do is traipse across the city when it's teeming with vampires."

"I'm right there with you, but someone spotted this guy near Marble Arch and I don't want to lose the one good lead I've had all week. If you don't want to go, I'll find someone else." She paused. "Normally I'd go alone, but as you said, the city is teeming with vampires."

Guilt washed over me. Of course she was anxious too. Just because I was a dhampir didn't mean I was the only one threatened by a surplus of vampires. Part of being a knight meant assisting the other members of the banner. We were a team. I'd even sworn an oath.

Argh.

"I'll help."

"Thanks, London. Meet you at Monument in half an hour. You're the best."

Maybe I needed to stop being the best. Then next time she'd call someone else first.

I WAS RELIEVED that Stevie wanted to meet at Monument because it kept me away from the heart of the celebration at Buckingham Palace. It also made it easier to arrive in half an hour because there were fewer crowds than normal and the bus was relatively empty. This area was even quieter than I anticipated. There were flags out in honor of the fallen queen, but no specific Britannia Day activity.

When I arrived, Stevie was pacing the pavement. She wore her suit of magical armor and combat boots. The armor's dark shade of blue complemented the silver undertones of her brown skin. Unlike the last time I saw her, the tips of her dark hair were bubblegum pink.

I gestured to her head. "What prompted the fashion statement?"

"Boredom."

"You need a special friend."

She cracked a smile. "From your lips to the gods' ears."

I surveyed the street. "Who are we looking for?"

"Caucasian male. White hair. Last seen wearing black trousers, a blue shirt, suspenders, and a bow tie."

"So we're hunting for an accountant."

She smiled. "Not quite."

We started walking toward the river. Stevie was a water witch so if the target decided to seek refuge in the Thames, he wouldn't get far.

"What did he do?"

"Stole from a client that owns a pawn shop. Judd's fallen on hard times so a thief is the last thing the poor guy needs."

"A pawn shop? What's valuable enough to get us involved?"

"The thief didn't take anything from the pawn shop. Judd was fishing with his son at a pond. The guy approached them under the guise of entertaining the kid with magic."

"And he stole from them right there and then? That's ballsy."

"He took the tackle box."

"He didn't take the rod?"

Stevie kept her gaze on the crowd, scanning for any sign of the target. "Apparently not."

"Why take the tackle box?"

"They're both infused with magic—the rod and the box. Apparently Judd shared this during their brief conversation. A wizard had dropped the items off at the pawn shop not too long ago and demonstrated how they work."

"And what? The rod guarantees a fresh catch and the tackle box always supplies worms?"

"More or less."

I grunted. "Sounds like a fairytale."

"There was a fire in the pawn shop a few weeks ago and

he lost a lot of inventory." She sighed. "His wife died last year as well as his brother, who was his business partner."

I blew out a breath. Talk about a series of unfortunate events. "What happened?"

"They received a tip on an estate in Mayfair and figured it was worth checking out. That was how their partnership worked. Judd worked in the shop and his brother sourced materials when foot traffic was low. Martha didn't usually leave the premises because of the children, but the estate sounded too big for Terrell to handle alone."

"It was a setup?"

Stevie nodded. "Vampire den."

Vampire dens formed when lower-class vampires were dissatisfied with their rations of blood and took matters into their own hands. They squatted in abandoned homes and banded together in their efforts to acquire blood by any means possible.

"They took over one of those grand houses in Mayfair. Judd said his brother didn't think twice about it because of the location. The vampires lured Terrell and Martha there with the promise of a treasure trove."

My whole body tensed. "I don't suppose Judd reported it."

"He considered it but decided he didn't want to draw attention to himself."

I didn't blame him. Once you were on vampire radar, it was hard to get off. Judd might've ended up in a worse position if the vampires decided he and his son would make good tributes. There'd be no justice for Terrell and Martha.

"So Judd's been trying to balance the shop with being a single dad and the business has suffered as a result," Stevie continued.

"The fishing expedition wasn't for sport then?"

She tucked a strand of pink-tipped hair behind her ear. "No. They were desperate for food." She pursed her lips, appearing to fight the unpleasant memory. "I know we're not supposed to make promises to clients, but I'm pretty sure I used the words 'if it's the last thing I do.'"

"How's he paying for our services?" He could've applied for a grant, but if he was trying to avoid vampire attention, then he'd want to find other means of payment.

"My choice from the pawn shop."

"Good deal." It really was. You never knew what you'd find in a place chock full of castaway objects.

Stevie's eyes flicked to the right. "Two o'clock."

I swiveled. A white-haired man stood in front of the building, deep in conversation with another man. They stood close together with their heads almost touching. The second man's head snapped up and he stared wide-eyed at the white-haired man.

I looked sideways at Stevie. "You didn't mention he's a wizard."

"I didn't know."

That added a layer of complication. We had to proceed with caution or we risked a public spectacle. No way would I create a public spectacle on a day when there were extra vampires afoot.

"Let's not go charging in," I advised. "Nice and easy."

Stevie cast a sidelong glance at me. "When do I ever go charging in? That's your style."

"It's more Kami, really."

The two men shook hands and the surprised man walked away. I wondered how much he'd lost in whatever bet they'd made.

"That's our cue," I said. I hurried over to the man before he latched on to another mark.

I adopted a friendly demeanor. "Hey, my friend and I were watching you from across the street. What kind of magic were you doing?"

"What kind do you think it was?" His grin was engaging and I found myself smiling back at him.

"Teleportation of objects," I guessed.

His gaze traveled from me to Stevie. "Snazzy outfits. Something tells me you're not here for a magic demo." He offered a hand. "The name's Bertram."

"London Hayes from the Knights of Boudica. This is my fellow knight, Stevie Torrin." I shook his hand. When I released it, I felt a small object in my palm. Queen of Hearts. "Well played, sir." I returned the card to him. "We're here to discuss a tackle box that you took from our client."

"Can't say I know anything about a tackle box. Can you describe it?"

Stevie gave me a hard look. "Can't I just get it through violent means?"

Bertram produced a bag of nuts seemingly out of thin air and offered us a handful.

I waved him off. "We're not interested in your nuts, thanks."

He grinned. "No worries. These are the only nuts I'd offer you."

"Give us the tackle box and we won't report you to the authorities," Stevie said.

Bertram smiled while continuing to chew. "You won't do that, my dear. If he were willing to get the authorities involved, he would've done it instead of hiring two third-rate knights."

Stevie squared her shoulders. "We're not third rate."

"Definitely not," I chimed in. "Second rate, maybe, but not third."

Bertram's hand darted to his pocket. Acting on instinct, I grabbed his wrist and jerked it toward me. Cards spilled from his hand and collected on the ground in a small heap.

"Sorry, I thought you were reaching for a weapon," I said. I stared at the items on the pavement. "Look, I don't know what you are, but I'm going to go out on a limb and say it isn't a wizard." A real wizard didn't need paraphernalia to perform magic.

Stevie scrutinized him. "You're human."

His face reddened and he stooped over to hurriedly collect his cards. "I'm a magician. Magic is right there in the name."

"A magician is nothing more than a trickster. You have no actual magic," Stevie accused.

"You've never heard of chaos magic, my dear?"

"Nice try. There's no such thing," I said. Bertram was clearly a grifter.

"Just because we haven't seen evidence of something doesn't mean it doesn't exist. Have we learned nothing from the Great Eruption?"

"Stop trying to distract us," Stevie said.

He stuffed the pack of cards in the front pocket of his trousers. "If the vampires believe I'm a wizard, then I don't need to register as a potential tribute. I'm excused."

"So you taught yourself enough tricks to pass as a mediocre wizard?" I asked.

"My father taught me. It worked for him." Bertram shrugged. "Sleight-of-hand was his specialty and he taught me from a young age."

I crossed my arms. "Let me guess. You started with pickpocketing and branched out from there." A modern-day Oliver Twist.

"More or less. Magic is a survival skill for me, same as for you, I imagine."

"Except my magic is real," I said.

Bertram gazed at me with a wistful expression. "Who's to say what's real and what isn't? Before the Eternal Night nobody would've believed vampires were real, yet they were."

"That's different. They were in hiding. Your magic isn't in hiding. It doesn't exist."

Stevie nodded. "What she said."

A sad smile formed on his lips. "My mother didn't like lying either. She registered like a dutiful citizen. On my sixth birthday, her number was chosen and she became a tribute." He gazed into the distance. "She never came home."

"And that's when your father decided you'd become a magician too?" I asked.

Bertram nodded. "Seemed like a sensible decision at the time. Still does."

"What happened to him?" Stevie asked.

"Oh, he died, but of natural causes. And he died knowing he'd done the best he could for me, which I'm sure made leaving me all that much easier."

It was impossible not to think of my mother. She'd felt much the same. She hated to leave me, but she died knowing she'd given me all the tools at her disposable to help me survive.

"You have to stop stealing, Bertram," Stevie advised. "The next knight who's sent to find you might not be as understanding."

He dragged a hand through his white hair. "What's a man like me to do? I've been practicing my brand of magic my whole life. I have no other marketable skills and I need to lay low to avoid detection."

I related to his predicament more than he knew. We both worked to hide our identities from vampires. At least I had actual magic on my side.

He popped a few more nuts into his mouth and chewed. "I considered becoming a knight once upon a time. Joining a worthy banner."

"What stopped you?" Stevie asked.

"I'd say it's the fact that he's not a wizard," I said.

"I don't care what you are," Stevie said. "Just hand over the tackle box and we'll be on our way."

Bertram regarded us. "You swear you won't turn me in to the authorities?"

"We avoid dealing with vampires whenever possible," I told him.

"Fine. I'll hand over the box if you promise not to report me or stop me from earning a living."

"I'd rather not make any deals. Just because I work for Judd doesn't mean I approve of you conning other people." Stevie looked at me. "How about you, London?"

I kept my gaze on Bertram. "Before I decide, I have one more question. Why didn't you take the fishing rod?"

Bertram squinted at me. "Because it was easier to take the tackle box. It had a handle."

"Bullshit. You had the chance to grab both and you only took one. Why?"

His gaze dropped to the ground but he remained silent.

"I'll tell you why," I continued. "You didn't want that child to suffer and you knew if you took it, he might starve to death. Yes, you stole, but you also showed compassion."

"I knew it would be easier for him to find bait on his own than fish, especially with an enchanted rod. I'm a thief, not a monster," he added softly.

Gods help me, I liked Bertram. I was getting too soft for my own good.

"Give us the box and we'll leave you alone," I said.

Relief softened his weathered features. He hurried to a bag that rested against the nearby wall and retrieved the tackle box from it. I hadn't even noticed the bag before. The color blended with the wall, which was likely a deliberate choice.

He handed the tackle box to Stevie. "Apologize to the man for me, will you? And his son."

"You could do that yourself," I said.

"I think not." He offered a wan smile. "And if you ever need to book a magician, you know where to find me."

Stevie took the tackle box by the handle as we walked away. "I'll take this to Judd right now."

"Good idea. I'll see you later."

She frowned. "Hey, where are you going? Euston is this way." She pointed.

"I'm not going to Euston. I'm going to Mayfair."

Stevie's eyebrows shot up. "No. Absolutely not, you maniac. You can't be serious."

"If I don't stop them, there'll be more casualties. Who knows how many people have already been killed by them?"

"Do you seriously think the authorities won't investigate the death of multiple vampires? You'd make yourself a target."

She was right. There was a certain amount of risk involved. On the other hand, the kind of vampires that lived in a den weren't a priority for the current regime. My trail would be cold by the time anyone got around to investigating.

"This is too risky even for you. Besides, it's Britannia

Day, remember? They're vampires. They're probably celebrating across town with the rest of them."

"Not these vamps." I knew their type. They weren't joiners. They were opportunistic leeches. "Which makes it the ideal time to strike. They won't be expecting it and there's less chance of the authorities responding quickly to any emergency calls."

"If you go to Mayfair, I swear to the gods I'll call the authorities on you myself. It's suicide."

I weighed my options. Truth be told I needed to make arrangements for my trip to Devon. Judd's wife and brother were killed a year ago. The vampire den might not be active anymore.

"Fine. I won't go."

Stevie's shoulders sagged. "Thank you. Now go home and get some rest. You look beat."

"Thanks for the compliment."

I turned away from her and headed toward Euston. I was so engrossed in my thoughts that I failed to sense the vampires until they were only half a block behind me. It wasn't the fact that they were vampires that was the problem. I was surrounded by city-dwelling vampires who had no reason to notice me. It was the fact that these particular vampires were following me. At first I thought we were simply heading in the same direction—until I turned to take a shortcut. They'd have no reason to take this route.

I quickly debated my options. They weren't being particularly stealthy and a cursory glance revealed they wore the uniform of the royal guard. Not random thugs then. I decided to take control of the situation and turned to face them. Two vampires—a redhead with a face as white as a marshmallow and a muscled brunette with a receding hairline. So much for superior vampire genes.

"You boys lost? I'm sure I can help you find your way if you tell me your destination."

"Your destination is the palace," the red-haired vampire said.

"On whose orders?"

"His Royal Highness, Prince Maeron."

I was momentarily startled. I would've expected Princess Davina or Prince Callan before the heir to House Lewis. I had no idea what to make of the order. Maeron was a wild card in the royal household.

"It's a holiday in honor of his mother. Isn't the prince busy with royal duties?"

The redhead angled his head. "You ask a lot of questions. Most people just obey orders."

Most people weren't killed because of their species.

I gestured to my magical armor. "Let me go home and change. I'm not dressed for a royal visit."

"Don't think he much cares," the brunette vampire said.

"Are you sure it was Prince Maeron and not Prince Callan?"

The vampires exchanged amused glances.

"We don't all look alike, you know," the redhead said.

"Pretty insulting," the brunette added. "For your sake, I won't repeat it in the palace as long as you come without a fight."

I held up my hands in acquiescence. An impromptu trip to a palace full of vampires at the request of a dubious prince.

What could go wrong?

6

I arrived at Buckingham Palace nestled between two vampire guards and with a medusa of knots in my stomach. Even if I'd had time to prep for the meeting, I'd be nervous about entering the lion's den on Britannia Day of all days. As we approached the palace, my body began to feel like someone was rubbing a cactus all over my bare skin.

"Where are the crowds?" I asked, noting only a few loitering vampires near the statue of Queen Britannia.

"Celebration ended two hours ago," the redhead said. "We had to miss the tail end of things to get our orders to find you." He sounded mildly resentful.

"If it makes you happy, I can toss scraps of paper over your head, step on your foot, and yell directly in your ear."

He glared at me.

"You don't like parades?" the brunette asked.

"No, not a fan of crowds in general."

"My sister's like that," he replied. "I can never get her to come out for Britannia Day. She'll go to a bar for drinks afterward, but she don't watch the parade or listen to the speeches."

A girl after my own heart.

The vampires stopped at the gate to discuss my arrival with the commanding guard on duty and he waved us through. Once again, nobody bothered to pat me down or take my weapons. It was a testament to their power rather than their stupidity.

I crossed the threshold into the palace and stifled a gasp of awe. Even on a repeat visit, the striking interior managed to render me speechless. Prior to the Eternal Night, the sprawling building was the official administrative residence of the House of Windsor, the last royal human family before the Eternal Night began. Once Queen B got her hands on it, she redesigned the entire interior and kept the layout a mystery to outsiders. Even if you were permitted inside, you were only privy to a view of certain public-facing rooms. And every one of those public-facing rooms was a shrine to the fallen vampire queen. Britannia portraits. Britannia statue. Everywhere you looked was a reminder of the triumphant vampire leader.

The vampires escorted me along an unfamiliar corridor.

"Where are we going?" I asked. I didn't like the idea of being taken somewhere new in the palace. For all I knew, my identity had been discovered and I'd end up in a dungeon until my execution.

"The prince requested you be delivered to his study," the redhead said.

"Prince Maeron has a study? Fancy that." He didn't strike me as a reader.

"You mock the prince?" the brunette said. "You're either brave or foolish."

"Can't I be both?"

My magic bucked against me and I took a few calming

breaths to soothe it. The faintest glow of silver right now would be a death sentence.

Prince Maeron glanced up at the sound of our entrance. With his thick head of chestnut-brown hair and dark eyes lined with thick lashes, he'd be considered handsome if it weren't for the perpetual scowl and menacing glint that suggested he'd not only kill you, but he'd enjoy it too.

"Leave us," he ordered.

The two vampires exited the room, closing the door behind them.

Woo-hoo. Alone time with a terrifying vampire. The stuff nightmares are made of. My day was about to end on a high note.

He gestured to the chair. "You may sit."

"Do I have to? I read that you can burn calories even standing still." I patted my stomach. "Core muscles are a wonder."

He arched an eyebrow. "There's that plucky attitude I remember. I suppose you're also weighed down by weapons that wouldn't protect you against me."

If he only knew.

"I'm a knight, Your Highness. Have weapon, will travel."

The corner of his mouth curved up in a half smile. "My spies tell me you were seen on Sloane Street. Why don't you tell me about your work for the pack?"

I was momentarily startled, although I shouldn't have been. Why wouldn't House Lewis keep eyes and ears on the city's major werewolf pack?

"What makes you think it's work-related? Maybe I was visiting friends."

His slight smile remained fix in place. It was a practiced expression, as though he'd watched himself in the mirror dozens of times—except that wasn't possible since vampires had no reflection.

"Come now, Miss Hayes. If I've learned anything about you, it's that your only friends consist of knights and the four-legged variety."

"Wolves have four legs. Besides, even if I were working for them, the specifics would be confidential."

"Not to me. In case you've forgotten, your entire livelihood is dependent upon our royal blessing."

How could I forget? The knights' license to practice magic came directly from House Lewis.

He rose to his feet and walked to the sideboard against the wall to my right. He was six-foot-two with the broad shoulders and regal air one would expect of a prince.

"If a wolf dies in our jurisdiction, the death must be reported. It is the law, or have you forgotten that as well?"

Damn. I'd give the vampire credit. His spies were good. Annoying, but good.

I chose my next words carefully, not wanting to piss him off. The prince was unpredictable and too much snark could result in cruel and unusual punishment. I was convinced that saving Davina's life was the only reason he tolerated my presence.

"Why are you interested in the pack?"

There. Nice and professional.

He raised a decanter from the sideboard. "Drink?"

"No thank you."

"It's whisky."

"Courtesy of House Duncan?" The snide remark slipped out before I could stop it.

He snorted. "As though I'd accept anything from that pathetic excuse for a vampire."

His derision was understandable. After all, the Highland King was responsible for the death of Maeron's mother.

"I never developed a taste for whisky," I said, maintaining a polite tone.

"I could have Adwin bring you wine instead."

"I'm fine, thank you."

"I hope you don't mind if I indulge myself then. It's been a long day. I would've put this meeting off until tomorrow given the holiday, but circumstances demanded I act now."

"Circumstances?"

As he removed the lid, it made a popping sound. "Of all the knights in the city, I found it curious the pack felt inclined to hire the very same knight who recently assisted our family." He tipped the decanter and poured golden liquid into a glass. At least it wasn't blood. "Perhaps I'm unduly paranoid, but I thought it prudent to inquire."

"You can rest assured the assignment has nothing to do with my work on behalf of your family."

He assessed me over the rim of the glass. "I'll be the judge of that."

There was no way I could stonewall the prince. I'd have to offer a few tidbits and hope it was enough. "There was an incident involving pack members and I happened to be present during it. That's why they hired me."

"The incident being the unreported death?"

"More or less."

He took a long, thoughtful drink. "And how can you be sure the incident wasn't pre-arranged?"

I choked back laughter. "If you'd been there, you'd realize how ludicrous that sounds."

His eyes glinted with an emotion bordering on anger. I'd insulted him. Oops.

"This is House Lewis territory and you are a knight. If

there was an incident involving the death of a local wolf, you are legally obligated to report the details to us."

I sucked in a shaky breath. I was caught between a rock and a hard place. If I told him the whole truth, I was betraying my client and risked the wrath of the werewolves. If I refused, I risked the wrath of the royal vampires. Not an ideal position to be in.

A knock on the door interrupted us and I thanked my lucky stars.

"What is it?" he yelled.

The door cracked open. "Your Highness, the princess has requested admittance."

Maeron's nostrils flared and he looked at me. "I had concerns your presence would make the rounds before we'd finished. If I'd become aware of the situation sooner, I would've arranged to meet you elsewhere, but I was worried I'd miss my chance to intercept you." He shrugged. "Some things can't be helped." He waved a lazy hand at the staff member. "Send her in."

Davina padded into the room in bare feet. The princess wore a pale pink dress that brushed the floor. Blond ringlets bounced around her head. She beamed at the sight of me, revealing a dimple in each cheek.

"I thought it was only a rumor, but I'm so pleased it's true. I wish someone had told me you were coming. Happy Britannia Day."

I smiled, although I couldn't bring myself to return the greeting. "It was spur-of-the-moment, Your Highness."

She squeezed my arm. "Oh, please. You saved my life, London. I'll always be Davina to you."

Maeron regarded her with a tense expression. "I'd like to know which staff member mentioned the knight's presence so that I may relieve them of their duties."

"Like I'd tell you." Davina wasn't remotely intimidated by her ruthless older brother. She settled on the loveseat and patted the empty cushion beside her.

I joined her on the loveseat and she swiveled toward me. "Tell me how you've been. Any exciting new assignments? I suppose you can't tell me, can you?"

Maeron's lips parted, revealing a set of dangerous fangs. "As a matter of fact, Miss Hayes and I were discussing that very subject."

Davina's eyes sparkled with interest. "No kidnappings, I hope. I'd hate to think of anyone in my situation. By the devil, the whole affair was horrid." She shuddered for effect.

"It's not a kidnapping." I could share that much.

"Just the other day I was telling Mother I might like to train as a knight."

"And I hope she reminded you that you are the heir to this House," Maeron said.

Davina turned to face him. "No, *you* are the heir to this House. I'm the window dressing."

"Davina, you sell yourself short," a familiar voice said.

My heart skipped a beat when a strapping vampire entered the room. Six-foot-four with taut muscles, dark blond hair, and green eyes that shimmered like two emeralds, he was a frightening yet magnetic vision. He moved with the grace of a jungle cat and I was equal parts drawn to and repelled by him.

Prince Callan. The Highland Reckoning. The Lord of Shadows. The Demon of House Duncan.

I hadn't seen him since my last visit to the palace when I purported to turn over the elemental stone to the king and queen. At that point, I wasn't sure I'd ever see him again. He seemed equally surprised to see me.

I started to rise from the chair. "Your Highness."

He motioned for me to sit and went straight for the decanter on the sideboard. "I didn't realize we had company. I'd have dressed for the occasion."

Maeron snorted. "What would that involve—shinier boots?"

"It's a shame Mother and Father aren't here," Davina said, oblivious to her brothers' posturing. "I'm sure they would have liked to see you, too."

I wasn't convinced her parents cared either way, but it was sweet that she thought so.

Callan swirled the golden liquid in his glass and took a sip. "I didn't realize they'd left the palace. Where are they?"

"Avoiding Britannia Day, of course. You know how Father is." She turned back to me. "He's not a fan of the limelight. We joke that if he'd gotten his way, vampires would still lurk in the shadows. He's more comfortable dwelling in obscurity."

"Must've been hard for him to be married to someone like Britannia then," I remarked with a note of sympathy.

Maeron wore a wry grin. "It's a good thing we can't see our reflections or Mother would've been too distracted by hers to win any battles. A reflective shield would've been a more effective weapon than any blade."

"Is that why she erected all those statues?" I asked.

He nodded. "It was the only way to see her likeness."

That explained the statues of Britannia without her king. If Casek had no interest in being the center of attention, he wouldn't want to see his image everywhere he turned.

"Don't forget all the paintings she commissioned as well," Callan interjected. "I had one in my bedroom until Mother asked the staff to remove it."

It wouldn't have surprised me to learn the placement

had been deliberate. Britannia had insisted on the prince as a hostage as part of the treaty eventually negotiated by Casek.

"You wouldn't have liked her," Maeron told his brother. "By all accounts, she was a difficult woman at the best of times. I don't know how Father didn't murder her in her sleep."

"Because apparently she slept with a dagger underneath her pillow," Callan said.

The queen really *was* paranoid.

Maeron clapped his brother on the shoulder. "Callan is our next Britannia. It's a wonder House Duncan was willing to hand him over. I can't think of any twelve-year-olds capable of leveling a city."

Callan could've leveled his brother with a single look.

"I'm not a wizard," he ground out. "I don't level buildings."

"No, but you emptied them of their inhabitants." Maeron paused to consider his words. "They really should've given you a better nickname. The Ghost of Birmingham perhaps."

"No alliteration," Davina pointed out. "It wouldn't have stuck."

"Highland Reckoning isn't alliterative," Maeron argued.

"No, but it has Highland in it, which instills fear," Davina said.

They both turned to regard her. "Does it?" they asked in unison.

Davina nodded. "It's only been twenty years and immortals have long memories."

"Only ten to go." Maeron raised his glass. "Right, brother?"

Callan lifted his glass in salute. "Perhaps, but this will always be home to me."

It never ceased to amaze how seamlessly the hostage has been integrated into House Lewis. Queen Imogen was his mother for all intents and purposes and he considered Maeron and Davina his siblings. He even referred to King Casek as 'Father,' which couldn't possibly go down well with King Glendon.

Davina beamed at her brothers. "Too right."

Maeron pivoted to me. "Did you know our favorite knight is now working on behalf of the West End Werewolf Pack?"

I wanted to take Maeron's glass and smash it over his head.

Callan looked at me with interest. "Is that so?"

"From what I can ascertain, she's investigating the unreported death of a werewolf," Maeron said. "I, for one, am dying to know more."

I would be more than happy to help him—with the dying part.

"Why was the death unreported?" Davina asked.

Maeron flashed an impish smile. "That's what I'd like to know."

"I'm not at liberty to divulge the details of my assignment. The banner has rules."

"And those rules are trumped by the law," Maeron pointed out.

Callan swirled the liquid in his glass. "What do you suggest we do, brother? Arrest her? Torture the information out of her?"

"Don't give him any ideas," I muttered.

Maeron swallowed the remaining whisky and set the empty glass on the sideboard. "Do not think your position is so secure with our House that you can flagrantly disobey the law."

"If you want more information, why not ask members of the pack and leave London out of it?" Davina asked. "She's only doing her job and you're making it difficult."

"Wolves kill each other all the time," Callan chimed in. "What business is it of ours?"

"That's what I'd like to determine. The pack wants to keep the death a secret. Why?" Maeron pinned me with a cool gaze.

"Because they're insular," Callan answered for me. "I'm sure they'd prefer to keep all matters within the pack if they could get away with it." He nodded toward me. "If facts come to light that impact this House or the community at large, I have every confidence London will do her civic duty."

Davina yawned. "It's been a long day and you must be tired from the festivities, brother. Why don't we leave London in peace?" She stretched her arms over her head. "I'm meeting Kitty and Beatrix tomorrow for brunch. If I don't look my best, there'll be gossip."

Maeron clutched his chest. "Heaven forfend."

I rose to my feet, grateful for Davina's intervention. "It was lovely to see you all again."

"Callan will escort you out." Before anyone could object, Davina looped her arm through Maeron's and practically dragged him through the doorway.

Callan and I looked at each other and a feeling of awkwardness washed over me.

"I know the way out," I said. "No need for an escort."

"I'm headed in that direction anyway."

I laughed. "The exit?"

"Actually, I'll show you a shortcut. That way you can avoid the guards."

"Why would I want to do that?"

"Because they make you uncomfortable."

And here I thought I was a master at disguising my feelings. I wondered what else he could tell. "Guards make everybody uncomfortable, especially those of us who aren't vampires."

"Fair enough."

He strode out of the study and I followed. Instead of turning left the way I'd come in, he turned right and then left at the next corner.

"The palace is a maze," I commented.

"You have no idea." He cut a sideways glance at me. "Is the pack job dangerous?"

"Don't know yet. I haven't started."

"My brother seems to think so or he wouldn't have summoned you here."

"I don't know the details of what his spies told him. I guess you'll have to ask."

A familiar figure emerged from a doorway and I recognized Adwin, the royal winemaker. In his arms he carried a crate of a dozen wine bottles. The vampire blanched when he spotted us.

"Good evening, Your Highness." He ducked his head. "Miss Hayes."

"Nice to see you again, Adwin."

"I was showing our guest to the private exit," Callan said. I thought it was interesting that he felt the need to explain.

I glanced at the room from which Adwin had emerged. The door was ajar and I glimpsed rows of bottles like the ones in the crate he carried. Maybe this was the storage area for the royal wine collection between delivery and the cellar.

The winemaker noticed my gaze and quickly hooked his foot around the base of the door to pull it shut.

"I'd love to chat," he said, "but sadly these bottles won't walk themselves to the cellar."

"Have a good night, Adwin," Callan called after him.

"How many storage rooms does the palace have for wine?" I asked.

Callan shrugged. "No idea. I don't concern myself with staff matters." He pointed ahead of us. "Third door on the left will take you to a tunnel that leads to the street."

My eyebrows inched up. "A tunnel?"

"More of a secret passage. No monsters."

"And no guards?" It seemed risky to leave an entrance to the palace unmanned. Queen Britannia would never have approved.

"Once you cross the threshold, you won't be able to get back in. It's warded so that only certain individuals can enter," he explained.

I couldn't imagine what kind of fool would want to enter the palace uninvited anyway. Even if you managed to make it inside, you'd be killed on sight. Guards patrolled the main sections of the palace and the royal vampires were powerful in their own right.

"I apologize for my brother's interference," Callan continued. "I'll have a word with him."

"You don't have to do that on my account."

"No, you can fight your own battles. I know. I've witnessed it firsthand." His smile was only faintly visible in the dim light of the corridor. "Sleep well, London. Perhaps our paths will cross again soon."

7

I awoke the next morning and began preparations for my journey to Devon. The most important step was making arrangements for the animals. As usual, Hera expressed her displeasure at being sequestered.

"It's for the best," I told the ornery cat. "I don't know how long I'll be gone."

No animal on earth glared like a cat. She added a flick of her tail for good measure.

I set up a summoning circle and sent the menagerie to the temporary realm I'd dubbed the holiday home where they'd be safe until my return. It felt good to release some of my magic. Sometimes the pressure got to be too much. I was a supernatural volcano on the cusp of my own Great Eruption.

Once the animals were squared away, I reinforced the ward to the pantry. If anybody managed to break through the exterior ward, which seemed highly unlikely, they'd be too spent to master a second ward. It helped that no one knew the stone was here. House Lewis believed they had the stone in their possession and no one else who knew of its existence would think to look for it here. I felt a twinge of guilt for deceiving Callan, but there was no way I was leaving a powerful stone that controlled elemental magic in the hands of vampires.

Next I packed a bag and debated the best choice of weapons. I needed to travel light so I opted for Babe, my axe, as well as Bert and Ernie, my two daggers. If those failed me, I had magic, although my license to practice didn't extend beyond the borders of House Lewis. I'd have to be careful. Avoiding magic was my preference anyway. The more I used in public, the more attention I drew and increased my chances of being discovered. If I wanted others to believe I was a witch with middling abilities, I had to play the part.

I locked the door, reset the ward, and headed to Paddington Station. Underground trains were nonexistent, but there were still a few functional overland trains that traveled between territories. For a trip to Devon, Paddington was my only option.

The station was surprisingly busy considering the early hour, but it made sense if most passengers were here for the Devon train. It only ran once a day so if you missed the morning train, you were out of luck until tomorrow.

Once inside the station, my vampire radar began to ping wildly. I straightened my shoulders and did my best to ignore it. I was about to be trapped for hours in a train carriage chock full of vampires. I couldn't let their presence unnerve me.

I surveyed the station. The area to show your ticket was first, then passport control. If you didn't have your pass to cross the border, you wouldn't be permitted on the train.

I purchased a roundtrip ticket and started toward the gate. A figure stepped in front of me, blocking my path.

"What's in Devon?"

I looked up into the bright green eyes of Prince Callan. What the actual...?

"You followed me here?"

"Guilty as charged."

I popped a hand on my hip. "When you said perhaps our paths will cross again soon, I didn't think you meant the very next day."

"It wasn't my intention, trust me, but it was either I follow you or Maeron sends his henchman." He paused. "Trust me. I'm the better option."

I motioned to the platform. "As you've surmised, I'm boarding a train to Devon, so if you're not prepared to cross the border, I don't think you're in a position to stalk me."

Callan turned to look at the train. "What's in Devon?"

"Confidential, remember?" I tried to brush past him, but he cut me off.

"Who authorized your pass?"

"I don't have a pass," I admitted. "My plan is to get my ticket checked and then turn invisible to evade passport control."

He frowned. "You can't be serious."

"What's wrong with that?"

"Aside from it being illegal, it won't work. You think you're the only one with the power of invisibility? Look around at all the vampires."

I'd rather not. "The odds of..."

He placed a warm hand on my shoulder and cut me off. "The odds are good that they'll catch you. They don't advertise it, but they have the means to do so."

So much for my plan.

The whistle sounded and a voice announced five minutes until departure.

"I can solve your problem," Callan said.

"You'll write me a pass?"

"Even better. I'll join you."

I laughed. "I don't think so."

"Why not?"

"Because I'm going to Devon on behalf of a werewolf pack, not House Lewis. And Devon, as you might recall, is neither in House Lewis or House Duncan territory."

"They don't need to know my true identity. I'll be a regular vampire traveling with my colleague on a professional assignment." He gestured to me.

"How do you expect to waltz into Devon? You're the Highland Reckoning. Someone will recognize you."

His eyes twinkled with amusement. "You didn't recognize me when we first met."

"I'm not typical."

He smirked. "No, you're certainly not."

I glanced over my shoulder at the train. The clock was ticking. "How do you expect to get us both through passport control if you conceal your identity?"

"You think I don't have the means to travel in secret?"

Another whistle sounded.

It was either this or postpone my trip until I obtained a pass through official channels. Romeo wanted me to be discreet and official channels tended to be slow and demanded too much information.

"Fine. Let's go."

His brow lifted. "Seriously?"

I urged him forward. "Get your ticket and move. The train's about to depart and it's the only one today."

I tapped my foot impatiently as Callan hurried to the ticket counter. I couldn't believe I was about to embark on a trip out of the territory with the Demon of House Duncan. What was I thinking?

Callan returned to my side wearing a smug grin. "Ready if you are."

"What about the passes?"

"O ye of little faith."

"Tickets, please," a vampire announced.

Callan and I showed our tickets. "Is there a particular carriage you recommend for the best views?" he asked.

"Left side for the sea on the way down. Right side on the way up." He shrugged. "Simple."

We waited our turn for passport control and I tried to keep my nerves at bay.

"Passes," the vampire guard said, snapping his fingers.

Callan produced two slips of paper seemingly out of thin air. The guard inspected them before handing them back.

The vampire tipped his hat. "Have a good trip, Mr. Lincoln. Ms. Washington."

"Lincoln and Washington?" I whispered as we headed toward the train.

He shrugged. "As a lover of history, I'm sure you can appreciate the choices."

"Wait a minute. Lincoln was the fake name you used when I first met you."

He grinned. "Like I said, do you think I don't have the means to travel in secret?"

I had more questions about these passes, but now wasn't the time.

He started to board and I placed a hand on his arm to stop him.

"This is first class."

"I'm aware. What's the problem?"

"My ticket is not first class. If you intend to accompany me, you'll have to forgo it. Will you survive the lack of legroom?"

His jaw set. "I'll manage."

We found two seats facing forward. I placed my bag on the overhead shelf and made myself comfortable.

"Have you ever traveled this light before?" I asked. He had absolutely nothing with him except his wallet. Then again, he probably carried enough money on him to remedy the lack of clothing and supplies.

"Only once," he said.

The train surged forward and my hands moved instinctively to the sides of the seat to brace myself. The move didn't go unnoticed.

"First time?" Callan's lips were touched by a faint smile.

I glowered at him. "No."

This was going to be a more stressful journey than I anticipated.

"Why did Maeron want to send his goons to follow me?"

"Why do you think? He desperately wants to know what the werewolves have you doing."

"I don't know how I'm going to explain to my client that a royal vampire insisted on joining me on assignment."

He leaned closer and whispered, "It'll be our little secret."

"Don't you have anything better to do? A bottle of wine to finish? A shop to ceremonially open?"

He burst into laughter. "Your idea of my daily life is quite divorced from reality, I assure you."

I turned to gaze out the window and watch the city roll by. Dingy gray buildings pressed against each other like sardines in a tin.

"Tell me about those fake passes," I said. "How often do

you sneak across a border with a woman that you carry them on you?"

Callan regarded me intently and I got the sense he was deciding how truthful he wanted to be.

"They're intended for emergency use only. One is for me and one is for Davina."

Wow. Not the answer I expected.

"What kind of emergency do you anticipate that involves you and the princess sneaking into another territory?"

The hard set of his jaw relaxed. "During the war, I witnessed families desperate to cross the border together just to get away from the atrocities." He shook his head. "Without passes, they were trapped." He paused and glanced away. "I never wanted that to happen to me."

"Then you became a hostage." You didn't get more trapped than that.

"That was different. That was for the sake of peace. A show of good faith on the part of House Duncan." He lowered his voice. "But if another House were ever to invade, I want to make certain I have the means to escape undetected. Once Davina was old enough to travel, I made sure to obtain a pass for her as well. I wouldn't leave without her."

It was obvious how much he cared for her and was completely at odds with his fierce reputation.

"You would flee rather than fight?" That admission also seemed at odds with his reputation.

"Depends on who's invading and why. I like to keep all my options open. Preparation is the key to success."

"Do you really think there's a chance another House will invade?"

He tilted his head back and closed his eyes. "If it happened once, it can happen again."

"If we fail to learn from history, we're doomed to repeat it. My mother said that all the time."

His eyes remained closed. "Your mother was a wise woman."

"Is part of the reason you'd prefer to flee because of what you witnessed during the war?" I knew it was a potentially inflammatory question, but I was curious about his view of events. It had to be incredibly hard, being the son of the invading king forced to participate in an attack. And only twelve years old to boot.

"The Battle of Birmingham was the worst day of my life," Callan admitted.

The vampire in the seat across the aisle turned to look at us. "Mine too. My parents were killed there." His fangs elongated. "Filthy little Highland bastard. I don't know why we spend tax money on keeping that monster alive. King Casek should've executed him on sight."

Beside me, I felt Callan tense and instinctively placed a hand on his thigh to calm him. The gesture was more intimate than I intended. His muscle tightened beneath my hand and I couldn't tell whether he was angry that I attempted to keep him in check or—something else.

"I'm sorry for your loss," I told him.

"Yeah, well. It was war, wasn't it? Everybody lost someone, not as catastrophic as the Great Eruption though." He stared straight ahead at the seat in front of him. "Now there was a time of absolute terror."

He went back to reading the book on his lap. Callan seemed to relax and I moved my hand back to my side. The last thing we needed was a fight to break out on a moving train and our identities discovered.

I turned my attention to the passing landscape, not that I could see very much of it in the gloaming.

Callan leaned closer. "If you want a stunning view, you should see Scotland."

I kept my gaze on the window. "Do you miss it?"

"The land and sea, very much. I spent many a night in the wild, not something I'm afforded in Britannia City."

"Your father liked to camp?"

He grunted. "Certainly not. I was accompanied by staff and my cousin."

"Are you two still in contact?"

The vampire hesitated. "He died during the invasion. Fought by my side until…"

And suddenly I understood. "Birmingham." I turned to look at him. "That's why you…you…"

He heaved a sigh. "I'm not proud of what I did, but I accept responsibility for it."

"You were grieving."

"The reason doesn't matter." He turned away. No wonder he didn't like talking about it. He wasn't proud of his youthful accomplishment. Of his immense power. Of his legacy.

He was ashamed.

I was so enthralled by his story that I failed to notice the signals my body was sending. "I need the restroom. I'll be right back."

Callan stood so that I could pass. I walked to the back of the carriage where the restroom was located. No wait. Perfect. I slipped inside and locked the door.

I emptied my bladder and washed my hands. One glance in the mirror told me it was time to relieve myself in more ways than one. My skin glowed with a faint silver light. Magic had a way of spilling out of me unless I used it in small doses to relieve the pressure. Too much magic and I risked being overwhelmed by it. Too little magic and the silver glow would give me away. I'd mastered the art of Goldilocks magic, thanks to my mother's training.

I turned on the tap and focused on the water. I tugged at the water molecules with my mind until they started rotating in the same direction. It took a certain level of concentration to keep the waterspout contained to the basin. I watched in admiration as the liquid funnel continued to spin.

A knock on the door interrupted me and the tiny waterspout fell apart and splashed across the sink.

"Hurry up in there. Some of us don't have bladders made of iron," a voice yelled.

I quickly checked my reflection and was relieved to see the silver light had faded. Back to pale beige.

I unlocked the door and smiled at the elderly woman. "Sorry about that."

When I returned to my seat, Callan gave me an appraising look. "Were they offering deep tissue massage in there? You look like you had a nap."

"I guess I really had to go. I feel much better now."

I settled against the seat and closed my eyes. If I was going to have the stress of a vampire companion on this journey, I was going to need all the rest I could get.

I awoke to the announcement of our arrival at the station.

"Welcome to Exeter, Sleeping Beauty," Callan said. "You really should do something about that snore."

"I don't snore."

The man with the book leaned across the aisle. "It was very quiet, like a soft motor."

My cheeks grew warm. No need to worry about silver now. My bright pink face would cover it.

I retrieved my bag from the overhead shelf and we

disembarked along with the other passengers. Once again, we had to show our passes to officers on the Devon side. The vampire on duty studied the passes for a beat longer than the one in Paddington, but handed them back to Callan without incident.

We left the station and I scanned the area for another mode of transport to reach Albemarle. A horse would be cheap but slow. A cab would be expensive and had the added disadvantage of a stranger behind the wheel who might take too much of an interest in us. There was a sign for car rentals, but growing up in the city, I never learned to drive.

"We should part ways now and plan to meet back here tomorrow for the return journey."

Callan laughed. "What makes you think I'd be willing to leave your side?"

"We both made it to Devon. You know my destination to report to your brother." I splayed my hands. "Seems like enough."

"When I said I'd join you, I meant it. You're in House Peyton territory now. You have no idea what to expect here."

"I'm a big girl. I'll figure out."

Callan blew out a frustrated breath. "I won't report the details to my brother. Whatever information you're gathering, I won't tell him."

"Then why stalk me at all?"

"To placate him. Maeron can be rather difficult when he doesn't get his way. Knowing him, he sent a backup spy to report on my actions." Callan pinned me with those emerald eyes and I felt my resolve weaken.

"If Romeo finds out, he'll make certain I never work in the city again."

"You saved my sister. I owe you my cooperation."

I stared at him for a moment, debating. It wouldn't be the worst thing in the world to have extra muscle with me in an unknown place. "Fine. I'll give you the background on the way there."

"This way." Callan began to walk with purpose toward the counter for car rentals.

"No. I can't drive."

"Then I suppose that's where I come in handy. Wait here."

He returned five minutes later with a set of keys and a satisfied expression.

"You seem pretty proud of yourself."

"You'd be amazed at what I can do."

We stared at each other for a beat too long.

He cleared his throat. "The car is parked over here."

It turned out to be a dilapidated, rusty jeep that looked ready for the scrap heap. I burst into laughter.

"That might get us a mile down the road."

He unlocked the doors. "It's more capable than it looks."

"Oh, then you two have something in common."

"We do. It's green like my eyes."

I frowned at the jeep. "It's black."

He barked a short laugh. "You're color-blind. It's very clearly green."

In a haze of gray, it was hard to discern the difference. I dug out my phone and used the flashlight feature.

"See? Black."

He slid behind the wheel. "It doesn't matter what color it is as long as it runs."

Suppressing a smile, I climbed into the passenger seat.

He started the engine and the lights came on automatically, a standard feature in a world of perpetual darkness. I tossed my bag on the backseat and snapped in the seatbelt.

"Don't you need directions?" I asked.

"I'll figure it out."

I groaned. Typical male. "I can tell you which way to go. I came prepared, you know."

He glanced at me. "If it weren't for me, you wouldn't have been able to get on that train, so I wouldn't gloat about your preparation skills."

We joined the road and headed south. According to the information I had, Albemarle was located on the edge of Dartmoor near a town called Ashburton.

"It's only about twenty-one miles," I said.

Of course, that was assuming we could take the A38, which was closed due to an accident outside Kennford, forcing us to switch to the A380. It was less direct, but it only added about fourteen miles to the trip—which would've been fine if the jeep didn't look ready to fall apart en route.

We made it as far as Heathfield when the engine began to smoke. Callan pulled off the road to investigate.

"It's overheating. We need water."

I glanced in the backseat to see a container. "That's probably what this is for." I lifted the container to find it empty. Terrific. "We passed a sign for a pond about half a mile back. It won't take long to go on foot."

"You have water magic. Can't you create enough water?"

"My magic doesn't work that way. I can manipulate what's there. I can't create it from nothing."

Callan bristled. "I'll thank my brother for this humbling experience later."

"You can stay with the jeep, Your Highness. I'm more than happy to retrieve the water on my own as your humble servant." I made a show of bowing my head.

He snarled. "And I'm sure you'll just happen to find your way to Albemarle without me. I don't think so."

"Fine. Do what you want." I retrieved my bag from the backseat. No point in tempting fate.

"I always do."

About two miles later, we arrived at a body of water.

"Looks more like a lake than a pond," I said.

He swiped the container from my hand. "Does it matter? Let's get on with it."

He crouched at the edge of the water.

I grabbed his arm and yanked. Hard. He landed on his backside.

The vampire snarled. "What the devil?"

"Don't look at your reflection!"

He frowned at me. "What's the matter? Worried I'll fall in love with myself and become a flower? I'm a vampire, remember? Can't see my reflection."

Okay, I'd acted on impulse. But still.

I pointed to the water where another face was now visible. Callan's eyes widened almost imperceptibly.

"It's a cochlea demon," I said. "If they get a lock on you while you're looking at your reflection, they can inhabit your body."

The vampire thrust a hand into the water and pulled the demon out by the scruff of the neck. The current body had shriveled beyond recognition. The demon spat a mouthful of water in Callan's face. The vampire simply blinked away the invading droplets.

"They're like snails," I explained. "They outgrow their host body and need to replace it with another one." Which meant they were always on the hunt for a body in good shape which Callan's most definitely was. In fact, the demon could live the rest of its unnatural life in a body like the vampire's.

Callan studied the demon as it writhed in his grip. "I feel sorry for the poor sod who gave his life to this thing."

"Don't throw it back in the water. It can't do any harm out here. It needs water to survive."

"It won't take long for it to crawl back to the lake if we don't kill it."

The demon hissed in response.

I debated the options. It seemed wrong to kill it when it was helpless. On the other hand, if we left it to kill another day, we were dooming another innocent life.

"We didn't pass any water between the road and here." Maybe there was a cave with a pool of water nearby. If the cave was secluded, there'd be little chance of someone wandering in there and peering at their reflection.

Callan frowned at the demon. "Are you certain that's what you want to do?"

The demon hissed, but the worst it could do in this position was spit. "Yes."

"Very well then." He tossed the demon over his shoulder like he was carrying a jacket. "Let's find a cave pool."

As I filled the container with water for the jeep, the demon decided to make its last stand and wrapped its desiccated arms around Callan's neck.

Big mistake.

The vampire flipped the demon onto the ground with preternatural speed. The demon's throat was slit before I had a chance to move. Thick purple liquid oozed from the wound.

Callan raked a hand through his dark blond hair as though surprised by the change in plans. "Some species have no sense of self-preservation."

"You were really planning to let it live, weren't you?" I asked.

He looked at me. "As a favor to you, yes."

Huh.

We walked the two miles back to the jeep in silence. RIP cochlea demon.

8

With a cooled engine and empty stomachs, we arrived at our destination.

Callan slowed the jeep to a stop in the middle of a long dirt driveway that led to the house. "This is Albemarle?"

The vampire sounded unconvinced. His misgivings were understandable. The house had seen better days. As Romeo mentioned, one side was missing an entire wall. Cracked windows. Crumbled stone. Missing shutters. Holes in the roof. The rest of the house wasn't in much better shape.

"Are you quite certain someone lives here?" he pressed.

"According to my client, yes."

Callan stared at the rambling country home. "I don't understand why anyone would live like this."

I thought of my adolescent years spent in the tunnels below Britannia City. "Probably because they have no other choice."

He parked the jeep outside the house and we exited together. We strode to the entrance and I knocked on the door that hung slightly askew. I glanced up to see the top hinge was broken.

A portly man greeted us at the door. His brown hair was combed to the side. He wore a black jacket and white shirt without a tie.

"Lord Bowman, I'm London Hayes and this is my associate, Mr. Lincoln. I understand you're expecting me."

The man offered a slightly amused smile. "I'm the valet, Grimsby. Lord Bowman awaits you in the study."

My eyebrows crept up. The house was in pieces yet the earl still employed staff?

We followed Grimsby through the massive foyer and I noticed a sparrow perched on the railing of the dilapidated staircase. It seemed to sense my attention because it chirped and flew away.

The flagstone floor was surprisingly clean considering the interior was somewhat exposed to the elements.

Grimsby stopped outside an open doorway. "May I present Miss London Hayes and Mr. Lincoln, my lord."

"Thank you, Grimsby." Theodore Bowman sat behind a large desk made of dark wood. He was a slender man of average height. The arm of his glasses was attached by a piece of clear tape that had been wrapped around multiple times. He wore a long-sleeved cotton shirt in dark green with a round neckline. His white hair was slightly disheveled and looked as though he might've trimmed it himself without a mirror.

I approached the desk with my hand outstretched. "Nice to meet you, my lord."

"A pleasure," he said, shaking each of our hands. "Please call me Theodore. I insist." He motioned to the threadbare chairs in front of the desk. "Sit down and we'll have a nice chat."

My butt wasn't padded enough to be comfortable on the hard seat. I'd endured much worse discomforts though.

"Tea?" he offered. "We're fortunate to have a selection. We can live without a wall but life without tea—is that even living?" His brow creased. "No sugar or milk, I'm afraid. No such luxuries at Albemarle." He didn't wait for our response. "Tea, please, Grimsby."

My gaze swept the large room. It would've been very grand once upon a time. The only evidence of it now was a shelf that spanned the length of the room lined with decorative blue plates.

"Lovely pottery," I said.

Theodore broke into a broad smile. "An incredible art form. Wouldn't you agree?"

I'd read enough history books to know that pottery had once enjoyed prominence during Ancient Roman times. It seemed to be enjoying a resurgence in the earl's household.

"I'm sorry my wife isn't well enough to join us," Theodore said. "She took to her bed earlier today with a headache."

"Is that unusual?" I asked.

"Not for Madeline. One of the pitfalls of dehydration. Not to worry. Our water supply will be repaired soon enough and Madeline will mend."

I worried about many things in connection with survival in the city, but my water supply wasn't one of them.

"I'm sorry to hear that."

It had been the sentiment I was about to utter but, surprisingly, Callan beat me to it.

Theodore emitted a small sigh. "Ah, well. You're not here to talk about our woes, are you?"

Grimsby entered holding a tray with a teapot and three cups on saucers.

"If you need the water, we're happy to forgo the tea," I said, although it seemed pointless to object now.

"It's boiled to death. Quite safe to drink," Theodore assured us.

"There's a contaminant issue?" I asked.

"Yes, but we'll work it out soon."

I used magic to filter the water in my flat, but I wasn't sure about an entire well for a house of this size. I'd need more information.

Grimsby offered us each a cup and I made sure to take a healthy sip. I wasn't about to waste precious resources.

"I understand you're in need of information. I'll help however I can," Theodore said. "It isn't often anyone requires my assistance. Nice to be needed for a change." There was a wistfulness in his tone that triggered a sadness in me.

"We're looking for information about berserkers," I said. "We understand this area was plagued with them until recently."

"It's the strangest thing. Incredible really." Theodore's eyes glazed over. "For generations the berserkers have been an issue for the people here. It's as though the storm blew them away."

All the way to Britannia City.

"Along with your wall," Callan remarked.

"Yes, a pity that. We were already struggling with repairs. The fallen wall's become one more burden."

I sipped the bitter tea, intent on drinking every last drop. I'd lick the inside of the cup if necessary. Anything to show the earl that he hadn't wasted his kindness on me.

"Tell us about the history of Albemarle," I said. "What kind of stones were used to build the house?"

He shrugged. "What's to tell? Same as any other grand house built during the same time period."

"And the wall was original to the house? It wasn't rebuilt at any point that you know of?"

He shook his head. "This house has been in my family for centuries, passed down from father to son. Like so many other humans, we fell upon hard times after the Great Eruption. My family fought to keep this place intact, but supplies grew increasingly expensive, as well as labor."

Britannia City seemed glamorous by comparison.

"You may as well take this back with you. It seems I no longer have need of it." Theodore removed a club-like object from the top drawer of his desk and passed it to me.

Callan regarded the weapon. "What is it?"

"It's called a wolf wand. Everybody has at least one in these parts. They're as necessary as a blade and far more effective against berserkers. If I'm close enough to a berserker to use a dagger, I'm as good as dead."

"I've seen one similar." Although Simon's was longer and more slender, closer in appearance to the wand of a witch or wizard.

"Where?" Callan asked.

It seemed unnecessary to hide the information from him at this point. He was on this mission with me whether I liked it or not.

"It was used at The Crown to subdue the wolves that went berserk. When we touched them with it, they reverted to their human form."

Callan turned his attention back to the earl. "Where do you get them?"

"A few people specialize in crafting them. They'll be out of business now if things carry on as they are. I probably held my first one when I was only a young lad. They've gotten better since then, of course. More expensive too, but such is life."

"Have you ever encountered a berserker?" I asked.

"Naturally. More times than I care to remember. Goodness, Madeline had a nasty brush with one just after the collapse of the wall. I was in town at the time. Madeline was outside and the wolf tried to speak but dropped to all fours and started to shift. Poor fellow seemed stuck. He snarled and thrashed and Madeline couldn't figure out if he was trying to attack her or ask for help."

"What happened?" Callan inquired.

"She retreated into the house for this." He held up the wand. "And then she waited to see if the wolf tried to enter the house. He stayed on the ground for quite some time, alternating between wolf and man. Madeline said it became too hard to watch and she finally closed the door and went upstairs. By the time I arrived home, he was gone. There were traces of blood but no sign of the rest of him."

Although it was harsh, I understood why Madeline left the wolf alone. It was impossible to know whether he would've attacked her, even if only as an outlet for his pain. She was right to stay indoors and protect herself.

"Was that behavior unusual for berserkers?" Callan seemed to be working something out for himself.

"They certainly don't wander to the front door like that," Theodore said. "They tend to stick to the woods. You learn which places to avoid on a walk."

"What about the shifting issues?" I persisted.

"I'm not aware of any quite so bad as that. The ones I encountered fell into the crazed wolf category rather than trapped between man and beast."

"Must've made it hard to venture out," I commented.

He shrugged. "You have your monsters and we have ours."

No kidding.

I studied the cornices on the ceiling. "This place has beautiful features."

"An absolute gem of a house," Theodore agreed. "I'd show you photographs of its glory days if you had more time."

The history scholar in me longed to see them, but the knight in me knew the clock was ticking. There were berserkers in Britannia City and Romeo Rice expected answers.

"Another time," I said with an air of promise.

"Where will you stay tonight?" he asked. "I can recommend lodging. I'd offer you a room here, but the only guest rooms are missing part of the roof."

"I'm happy to take suggestions," I said.

"There's a wonderful place called Bramblemoor that I highly recommend. It's not far from here and the widow could use the business. Her husband died during a routine donation a few months ago."

"A donation?" I repeated. "He was a tribute?"

"Yes. If I'd given it more thought, I would've chosen someone else. I hadn't been thinking of Bramblemoor, only that Mr. Merton was a healthy man with no known impairments."

I frowned. "What do you mean you would've chosen differently?"

"Ah. The system works differently here, I suppose. Everybody registers." He paused to slurp his tea. "But I select the tributes in this area. One of the perks of earldom."

"*You* decide who donates blood?" I couldn't imagine the weight of that responsibility.

"I choose carefully, of course. House Peyton can be... touchy if they feel they've received less quality than they deserve." Theodore smiled at Callan. "No offense. Vampires must have their needs met, of course."

No wonder he wanted us to spend money at Bramblemoor. He had to feel terribly guilty.

"Does House Peyton mind that you've retained your title?" Callan asked.

Lord Bowman shrank back, appearing stunned by the question. "Why on earth wouldn't I retain it?"

"Because you're human in a world ruled by vampires." Callan kept his tone matter-of-fact, but I had no doubt the vampire had opinions on the subject.

"My family has had the privilege of overseeing this land for centuries," he said, drawing out the words slowly and carefully. "I'm proud to carry on the tradition."

"What other benefits does it provide? Aside from offering people other than yourself as part of the buffet?" Callan seemed intent on pressing the earl's buttons now, which I didn't appreciate. I had work to do and a distressed earl would only make my job more difficult, not that Callan cared. He was only here because Maeron was nosy and he had nothing better to do with his unfettered time.

"Mind your tongue when you're a guest in my home," a red-faced Theodore sputtered. "I'm a member of the nobility and I deserve respect even from a vampire."

My gaze swept the crumbling interior. It seemed strange to cling to a title that served no purpose. Theodore was clawing at empty air and expecting to find a gilded rope swinging there just for him.

Callan eased back against his chair. "Apologies. I meant no disrespect."

"Apologies, *my lord*," Theodore said.

Hesitation flickered in Callan's eyes. It was obvious the prince in him wanted to refuse and display his peacock feathers. I clenched my hands into fists as I waited to see how he would respond. The earl would be looking at a second missing wall if he wasn't careful, not that he had a clue as to Callan's real identity.

"Apologies, my lord," Callan said with a polite smile.

I relaxed. Crisis averted.

An older woman wandered into the study in a white nightgown that reached her bony ankles. Her complexion was a shade paler than Theodore's and her eyes had the glazed look of someone who'd seen more in her lifetime than her mind could process.

Theodore smiled at the sight of her. "Madeline, my dear. You're up. How splendid."

Neither husband nor wife seemed remotely bothered by her attire.

"I'm so sorry," she said, her voice barely a whisper. "I didn't realize we were entertaining guests."

Callan and I stood to greet her.

"London Hayes, Knight of Boudica," I said, and shook her hand. Her fingers were limp in my hand. "This is my associate, Mr. Lincoln."

Madeline smiled up at Callan, the slight tinge of pink returning to her cheeks. "How lucky for you to travel with someone so...clearly capable."

I bit back a smile.

The compliment sailed right over her husband's head. "I would love to travel," Theodore said. "If only we didn't have so many responsibilities anchoring us here."

If you couldn't afford to repair your wall or fix your water supply, a seaside adventure in Cornwall was likely out of the question.

"I don't suppose you'd be any good with repairs to our water supply," Madeline said, keeping her gaze pinned on

Callan. She seemed to mistake him for a white knight to the rescue.

"Is there no one local?" Callan asked.

Madeline scowled. "There's a witch with elemental powers who could easily remedy the situation but she refuses to help. Selfish cow."

"Now, dearest," Theodore soothed her. "You know why Brumhilda has no interest in helping this estate."

My eyebrows shot up. "Seriously? Your local witch is called Brumhilda?" It sounded like a name straight out of a fairytale, the kind of name a witch was given by someone who'd never met a real one.

Madeline crossed her arms and glared at her husband. "She ought to let bygones be bygones."

Now I was too curious to let it go. "What happened?"

"We insulted her," Theodore said simply.

I snorted. "How? You didn't invite her to your baby's christening?"

Theodore tipped back his cup and finished the remaining droplets of tea. "Madeline declined to purchase certain beauty products."

"She makes them herself," Madeline added. "I don't like the idea of using a lotion on my skin that she mixed in her cauldron." She shivered. "What if she put something in it that allowed her to control me? What if she uses magical face cream to suck out people's souls?"

Callan and I exchanged amused glances. "She's a witch, not a demon," I said.

"I mean no disrespect to witches," Madeline said. "It's just that Brumhilda is a bit...strange. And pushy." Madeline flapped her slender arms. "I have a roof caving in and a missing wall. Do I seem like someone in need of lip liner?"

I shrugged. "If that's how she earns her living."

"She could earn a living by using her elemental powers to repair our water supply," Madeline said.

I debated whether to offer to repair it myself. I might be able to manage it. Then again, it seemed smarter to mend the broken fence between the two parties. The Bowmans had a better chance of survival with an elemental witch on their side.

"Why don't I speak to Brumhilda on your behalf?" I offered. If the witch refused, then I'd see if I could use my own magic. Callan already knew about my water magic thanks to a tussle with a selkie in Hyde Park, so there was no need to hide it from him.

"You would do that?" Madeline asked.

"Yes. In return, I'd like a list of everyone who came here to help you after the storm."

A mild chuckle followed the request. "I couldn't possibly tell you that," Theodore said. "I didn't pay attention."

"But it's possible someone else in the household did. Grimsby, maybe?"

"You're welcome to ask him." His brow furrowed. "What's this got to do with berserkers?"

"I'm not sure yet," I said truthfully. "I'm simply collecting information."

"For goodness sake, she's going to speak to the witch. Give her whatever she needs," Madeline insisted.

Theodore nodded. "Of course, my love."

"You can find Brumhilda in a cottage two miles south of here as the crow flies," Madeline said.

I resumed a standing position, grateful to give my backside a rest from the hard surface. "Thank you. Before we go, I'd also like to take a look at the wall from the outside if you don't mind."

Theodore motioned to the doorway. "Be my guest. Just

don't abscond with any supplies like some of the hooligans we've chased off the property. We need every rock we have."

"Wouldn't dream of it."

"I'll have Grimsby meet you outside with a list," Theodore said.

Callan and I left the house unescorted and wandered around to the gaping wall.

"Interesting family," he remarked.

"Dragonflies in amber," I said. The Bowmans were stuck in a life that no longer existed.

Callan tossed a wayward rock aside. "Quite a storm they had."

I observed the pile of rocks that now served as the fourth wall. "No kidding."

"Too bad these aren't all elemental stones," Callan joked. "Then they wouldn't have to deal with Brumhilda. They could repair the water supply. The wall. Everything."

I started to laugh but the sound died in my throat.

Callan noticed my mixed reaction. "What is it?"

I picked up the nearest stone and hefted it in my hand. "What if that's what we're dealing with?"

"It obviously isn't. The elemental stone only controls the elements, not shapeshifting. Besides, it's safe at the Tower with the immortality stone."

My mind was racing. It hadn't occurred to me there might be another kind of stone in addition to the two we knew about.

I studied the plain stone in my hand.

What if there were more?

The question was too overwhelming to contemplate.

Grimsby rounded the corner clutching a sheet of paper. "The list you requested, miss."

"Thank you." I accepted the paper. "If you think of

anything noteworthy that happened around the time of the storm, will you let me know?" I retrieved a business card from my pocket and handed it to him.

"Yes, miss. Of course." He turned and scuttled back to the house.

Callan was staring at me. "What kind of stone would cause shifters to go crazy?"

"No idea, but think about it. There's been a history of berserkers in this specific area for centuries. Even before the Great Eruption, there were reports of rabid wolves that attacked travelers here."

Callan nodded. "And then the storm blows through, knocks down the wall, and suddenly they're gone."

"And wolves in Britannia City who were otherwise normal before are now acting like berserkers, which means they weren't born berserk. It suggests they were influenced by an external source."

Callan patted a loose stone. "Why would anyone bring a stone from here to Britannia City?"

I wasn't sure. "Maybe they sensed it had power, but they didn't know what kind. If it's anything like the other two stones, it would have markings."

Callan whistled. "I hate to admit it, but I think you're on to something.

But what kind of stone controlled the ability to shift?

"We need to find a local berserker," I said.

"Even if we find one, who's to say they'll be able to communicate with us? They were stuck as wolves their whole lives."

And not just any wolves. Wolves that were out of their minds.

"It's worth a try."

He tossed a stone back on the pile. "Let's go then."

"Brumhilda first."

"Somehow I knew you were going to say that." He hopped into the driver's seat. "Is this part of being a knight or is it just you?"

I closed the passenger door and looked at him. "Is what?"

"The helpfulness."

I clicked my seatbelt into place. "My mother always said no act of kindness, no matter how small is ever wasted." I paused. "Actually, Aesop originally said it, but my mother quoted him a lot."

"She was a learned woman, your mother?"

"Very." Unlike me, who now had a list of names but far more questions than answers.

9

Down a dirt path and nestled amongst the trees, Brumhilda's cottage was relatively easy to find. The hot pink neon sign on the side of the road that spelled out *Brumhilda's* and pointed us in the right direction probably helped.

And the blinking neon sign on top of the thatched roof of the cottage with an arrow that pointed downward.

Callan parked the jeep and I unbuckled my seatbelt. "I think you should wait here."

He grinned. "You're worried about someone stealing the jeep and being forced to spend the night?"

"I'm worried that Brumhilda won't appreciate a vampire on her doorstep and turn us both away."

His smile faded. "But I'm…"

"Exactly. What if she recognizes you?"

"Then she'll be more inclined to let me in."

"And she might be inclined to report your presence to House Peyton to gain their favor."

He tapped his fingers on the steering wheel. "I see your point."

"Take a scenic drive while I'm gone."

I closed the door and approached the cottage. A small brown and white animal scurried behind a dark green pot that would've once served as a decorative planter. I caught sight of the short tail as it disappeared.

As I lifted my hand to knock on the door, the animal's head popped out from behind the pot. A weasel.

"Hey, friend," I said.

I reached out to touch the animal's mind and see whether the vibe was friendly. I quickly withdrew when I felt a second presence. She wasn't a random weasel.

"You're a familiar."

Not all witches had them so they weren't as common as they once were. They seemed to fall out of fashion at some point during the Eternal Night, most likely because witches were too busy struggling for survival to care for a companion. My mother never had one and neither did I. Barnaby was the closest thing I had to a familiar, but we didn't talk to each other in the traditional sense. I was unusual in that I could form a bond with almost any animal I chose. I didn't need a familiar in the same way another witch might.

The weasel crept out from behind the pot and watched me with interest.

"Throw a girl a bone," I told the weasel. "Am I about to get roasted and have an apple shoved in my mouth or what?"

The weasel trilled.

"Thanks." If she'd hissed or chirped, I would've been more on edge. A trill was a good sign.

I rapped lightly with my knuckles on the wooden door.

"Come in!"

The door creaked open and I poked my head inside. The interior of the house was as small as my flat but crammed full of...stuff. There were cushions in a variety of shapes and colors. Pink leopard print blankets were tossed over every available surface and the floorboards were covered by multiple rugs that appeared to have no colors or patterns in common. Tennis racquets, framed maps, and watering cans adorned the walls as objets d'art. A disco ball hung from the low ceiling, catching the fragments of light that flickered from the lit candles. The style could best be described as indoor junkyard meets casino chic.

A woman stood beside a large black cauldron that was tucked in an Inglenook fireplace. Her lavender hair was streaked with white and she wore it rolled in a thick bun at the base of her neck.

"Brumhilda, I presume?"

The witch barely looked up from her cauldron. "Just a second. If I don't time this properly, I'll ruin the whole batch and have to start from scratch."

She tossed a few seeds in the mixture and gave the whole thing a final stir before setting down the spoon.

"Who are you and why does Winnie seem to like you so much? She doesn't like anybody."

I looked down to see the weasel had accompanied me inside. Slick little creature.

"My name is London Hayes."

Suspicion gleamed in her eyes, which were accentuated by thick black mascara and smears of light purple powder that sparkled. Upon closer inspection, I realized her skin was coated in a fine layer of foundation that matched her bronzed skin tone. Coral lipstick covered the cracked skin of her lips.

"I don't know anybody by that name," she said. "It's a strange one at that."

"That's a lovely shade of lipstick."

"It's called seashell. I made it myself."

"Is that what's in the cauldron?"

She glanced at the cauldron as though noticing it for the first time. "Dearie me, no. That's a protein shake."

Right. "I've come on behalf of the earl and his wife."

Grimacing, she turned back to her cauldron. "Then you can find your way out again."

She wouldn't get rid of me that easily. "Nice place you've got here."

"It is, isn't it? And I have all four walls plus a full roof unlike *some* people." She peered at me. "Which part of Devon are you from? I don't recognize your accent."

"Because I'm not from Devon. I bet the rent's cheap in this part of the country though."

She spat on the floor. "Rent. What would I know of rent? I own everything you see. If I can't own it, I don't have it. Simple. I'm not beholden to the so-called earl or House bloody Peyton or anyone else."

"An independent woman. I can appreciate that."

The witch rested a hand on the lip of the cauldron. Steam wafted past her arm and I watched to see whether the heat scalded her. If so, she didn't show any pain.

Interesting.

"So what does the earl need from me when he's clearly found himself another witch?"

I saw no reason to lie. "I wasn't called upon by the earl. I went to see him about an unrelated matter on behalf of a wolf pack in Britannia City."

"That explains the accent." With the flick of her finger, the fire beneath the cauldron died. "Do you know the kind of magic I possess?"

"Do a few more tricks like that and I can probably piece it together."

She looked me up and down. "A smart mouth. We don't get a lot of those around here. Must be the city's influence."

Or the risking-my-life-every-day influence. You don't tend to watch your tone when you're battling monsters on the regular. Each word might be your last. You might as well increase the odds of making it a good comeback. Kami and I used to laugh about what might be written on our tombstones. It was easy to joke when you knew you'd never have one.

"Based on the Bowmans' desire to have you fix their water supply and the fact that you kept your hand on a hot cauldron without burning yourself, I'm going to go out on a limb and say you're an elemental witch."

Her smile revealed a set of surprisingly straight white teeth. "I possess all the elements. A rare gift."

"All?"

She counted them off on her fingers which were adorned with rings. "Earth, air, water, fire."

Not all then. She didn't seem aware of the ancient metal that formed the fifth element, Damascus steel—a recent discovery along with the elemental stone. Still, four out of five wasn't too shabby for a witch in the middle of nowhere. No wonder her abilities were in high demand.

Brumhilda narrowed her eyes. "If you're going to have contrary thoughts, you should do a better job of hiding them."

"Are you telepathic?"

"No, but your poker face needs work." She angled her head. "What is it that you long to tell me?"

"Nothing. I was impressed by the range of your abilities. I'm a knight and even our elemental witches tend to specialize in only one or two."

Brumhilda's smile broadened. "More impressive than a

knight, am I?" She gestured to the square table with its two wooden chairs that would give even the strongest back a terrible ache after too long. "Why don't you sit and tell me about these knights of yours? We'll compare notes."

I sat at the table with my back to the door, my least favorite position but the only other option was the chair the witch had already chosen for herself.

"Would you like a drink? Or perhaps a bite to eat? I'm a bit peckish myself." She glanced at the shelf in the kitchen with its rows of jars. "How do you feel about jam and bread?"

"I'm fine, thank you."

Her mouth formed a thin line. "In this part of the world, it's considered rude to decline your host's offering."

"Even if it's disgusting like a hairy eyeball?"

She blew a breath. "There's no such thing as a hairy eyeball."

"There is if you know the right spell."

"Why would anyone want to grow hair on an eyeball?" She shook her head. "Such a waste of magic."

"I'm traveling with a companion and I'd rather not eat without him." I had no appetite in a place where I felt uncomfortable. It didn't exactly reek of danger, but I didn't feel as though taking a nap would be a smart move either.

Brumhilda pushed back her chair. "Suit yourself." She shuffled to the kitchen and poured herself a light golden liquid from a pitcher. Then she took a saucer and used it as a small plate, adding cubes of bread and a ramekin of purplish jam.

"Why don't you like the Bowmans?" Might as well get straight to the point. The sooner I resolved the issue, the sooner I left the witch's scrutiny behind.

"What did they tell you?" She returned to the table with her glass in one hand and the saucer in the other.

I recounted the Bowmans' version of events.

Brumhilda scoffed. "Lies. Every word." She pushed the saucer across the table but I shook my head. Pulling it back toward her, she said, "I'd say they were manipulative, but honestly they're too stupid. They're just bumbling fools."

"So you'd let them die of dehydration as punishment?"

She shrugged. "Why not? They serve up their people on a platter for House Peyton to save their own skin."

"How does that impact you? You're a witch. They can't offer your blood."

She squinted at me from over the top of her glass. "Do things only matter to you when they only impact you directly?" She didn't wait for my reply. "No, I think not." She took a long drink and set down the glass. "You wouldn't be here now if you lacked compassion."

"I'm here on a job. I'm being paid to be here."

She snorted. "You can tell yourself that, my dear, but I sense there's more to you than being a mercenary."

"I'm a knight."

She ran her finger around the rim of her glass. "Same difference."

I found I lacked the will to argue the point.

She looked down her powdered bronze nose at me. "Why don't you help them if you care so much about their fate?"

"You're local. I think it makes more sense for you to do it. Build a sense of community."

"Is that truly the reason?" The witch looked at me with an intensity that made my skin crawl. It was suddenly like she saw straight through me to my innermost secrets—

secrets I couldn't risk being uncovered by anyone, least of all a witch with no reason to protect me.

"I have no idea what you mean."

She laughed. "Come now, my dear. I hate when women play stupid. It demeans the entire gender."

"Gender is a construct."

I was relieved by my decision to leave Callan behind. Brumhilda was clever. She would've sniffed out his identity in a heartbeat.

"The earl believes himself to be more important than he is. It irritates me."

There. Now we were getting somewhere.

"He owns a lot of land for someone unimportant."

"Yes, but you've seen the state of his house."

"Hence his need for your services."

She shrugged. "It isn't unusual in this part of the country to find a great house in disrepair," she explained. "Families like his are landed gentry clinging to a world that no longer exists."

"Which explains the valet."

"Bless that Grimsby. They can no longer afford the upkeep, but Albemarle is Lord Bowman's ancestral home and he refuses to leave it."

"Even if someone with deeper pockets could come along and salvage it?" If the earl viewed himself as merely a custodian of something bigger than himself rather than an owner, you'd think he'd be more than willing to see it restored to its former glory by another.

"Bah! The only ones with pockets deep enough would be vampires and he'd rather die than see fangers occupying the family estate. They already own most of the great houses they haven't destroyed."

To some degree, the earl's reluctance was understandable. Even with the walls crumbling, where would he go that was better? In this world, every home had its dangers. A high-rise in Britannia City increased the risk of encountering dragons or other flying monsters. A cabin in the woods exposed you to shifters and demons passing through. The safest place I could think of was Buckingham Palace and that was only if you were a royal vampire. I certainly wasn't safe in a house like that.

"What can you tell me about the berserkers?"

"Oh, good. A change of topic." She played with a false eyelash that had wandered too close to its neighbor and gotten stuck. "There've been berserkers in this area for as long as there have been wolves, until very recently."

"You don't seem particularly surprised by the change in circumstances."

"When you've been alive as long as I have, very little surprises you."

"And how long is that? It's hard to tell."

She smiled as she managed to separate the eyelashes. "The results are astounding, aren't they? Takes years off my real age."

"What kind of magic do you use in the cosmetics?"

"Very subtle earth magic. You'd be surprised what it can do. Such magic is far more versatile than we realize."

No kidding.

"If you really want to know about the berserkers," she continued, "you should ask House Peyton. They're vampires, after all. If anyone knows the history of this territory, it's them."

"But they haven't been here for centuries. Not personally." Vampires were immortal, but they could be killed and often were. And like Callan, not every vampire was hundreds of years old.

The corners of her mouth curved upward. "Not interested in that option, are you, sweetness?"

"I don't think either one of us would be."

The witch's smile dissipated. "You've got that right. A miserable world this is, shrouded in darkness. Why do you think I surround myself with bright colors?"

"I thought those signs outside were more for practical purposes. To attract customers."

"That, too."

I had one more question for her. "Can you point me to any wolves who were berserk before the storm but are now...normal?" For lack of a better word.

"I couldn't tell you any of their names," she said. "But I can tell you where you might find one." Her gaze drifted to the window. "The moor. Where the River Dart meets the River Webburn. When you pass through a village called Mirth, you'll know you're on the right path."

"Thank you. That's helpful." I hauled myself to my feet.

"Can I interest you in any cosmetics before you go? A beautiful face like yours doesn't need much, but a touch of lipstick and mascara would enhance your assets."

I patted the axe strapped to my back. "This is the only asset I need."

"Just because we're independent women doesn't mean we should be alone. I imagine you crave company once in a while."

"The only thing I crave is a good night's sleep so I can work the next day without making a fatal mistake."

"Your eyes betray you," she said. She splayed her hands on the table and pushed herself to her feet. "I'll fix Albemarle's water supply."

I straightened. "Really?"

"Yes, but only because I don't want new neighbors. If

they're forced to leave, vampires will be the only ones in a position to take on a house of that size and I don't want the bloodsuckers any closer than they already are."

"Then maybe you could use some of that versatile earth magic to help repair the wall."

She scowled. "Why do I care whether they get wet from the rain?"

I threw her words back at her. "Do things only matter to you when they only impact you directly?"

Her scowl deepened. "Be on your way, knight, before I change my mind."

I found my way to the jeep that was idle by the roadside. Callan leaned across to open the door for me.

"Well?"

"We need to go where the River Dart meets the River Webburn." I strapped myself into the seat.

"Because you're going to repair the water supply?"

"No, because that's where we might find a former berserker. There's a village called Mirth nearby."

He swung the jeep around and joined the road. "Unfortunate name."

It didn't take us long to find the route to Mirth. It was an isolated area and the village itself was quiet. Unlike the kind of ominous silence that indicates something wicked this way comes, the current quiet was comfortable. A place and its people at rest.

Callan parked the jeep in front of a general store.

"What are you doing?" I asked.

"Thought it might be a good time to stock up on supplies."

"You couldn't have done that while I was busy with Brumhilda?"

He climbed out of the jeep. "I didn't want to stray too far in case you needed help."

"How many times do I need to tell you...?"

I didn't get to tell him again. A bearded man stepped around the corner with a pistol aimed at me. "Not another step, thief." His gaze landed on Callan. "Thieves, plural. You've taken quite enough from us. There'll be no more."

Callan and I exchanged glances. Slowly I raised my hands so the man could see they were empty. "We're not here to take anything."

The man narrowed his eyes in suspicion. "No? I suppose you're all stocked up now."

I pressed the heel of my boot on Callan's foot to stop him from launching himself at the bearded man. One sudden move from the vampire and the man would surely shoot.

"We haven't been here before," I said, maintaining eye contact with the stranger. "We're only passing through on our way back from Albemarle and decided to stop for supplies."

He squinted at me. "What business have you got there?"

"I believe that's *our* business," Callan told him.

"If you lower your weapon, we can talk." I tried to keep my voice gentle and friendly, although it wasn't easy when I wanted to rip the pistol from his hand and beat him on the head with it. Thanks to my upbringing, my survival instincts were stronger than my manners.

"Do I look a fool to you? If I lower my weapon, you'll steal my gun and whatever else you choose."

"Where did a man like you even get a gun?" Callan asked.

The man's eyes popped with indignation. "A man like me? What's that supposed to mean? I don't look important enough to you? Is that why you feel entitled to waltz in here bold as you please and take our livestock?"

"We haven't taken any livestock. I'm a knight from Britannia City." I wiggled my fingers. "I can show you proof, but I don't want you to think I'm reaching for a weapon."

The man almost smiled but seemed to catch himself. "You're a knight?" He shifted his aim to Callan. "Both of you?"

"No, this gentleman is my client, Mr. Lincoln. That's why we were at Albemarle together."

The bearded man inched closer. "The gods must have sent you to us. We can use a knight in the village. We can even offer you food and shelter in exchange for your help."

"What makes you think the thief will come back?" I asked.

"In the past fortnight, two cows and three pigs have been taken, along with a carriage." His brow wrinkled. "The livestock I can understand, but the carriage wasn't much good to anybody. It had been in Nina Stark's barn for years."

"Not a huge loss then," Callan said.

"No, but she also owned two of the pigs that were stolen."

"And you owned the rest?" Callan inquired.

Confusion marred the man's features. "No, sir. Sherman owned a cow. The third pig belonged to the Scotts."

I understood the bearded man's involvement. In a place like this, the cows and pigs didn't simply feed the families that owned them. They serviced the entire village.

I angled my head. "Why don't you lower your weapon and we can talk more about it?"

He glanced at the gun as though he'd forgotten it was there. "Yes, of course." He lowered his arms to his sides and tucked away the pistol. "The name's Rochester."

Callan gaped at him. "You haven't checked her credentials."

Rochester's eyebrows knitted together. "You don't believe her?"

"No, of course I do. I'm traveling with her, aren't I? It's just that you're taking her word for it. You should be more discerning."

Rochester scratched his head. "So you think I should take the gun back out?"

Callan groaned. "Forget it."

"Is there somewhere we can talk?" I asked.

Rochester jabbed an elbow to the side. "This is my store. We can talk inside."

"So what makes you believe the thief will strike again?" I asked, once we were inside the general store. It was a small building with a mishmash of supplies. It had everything from soap to bottles of ale.

He leaned an arm on a nearby shelf. "Don't see why they'd stop. They've been getting away with it and there's more to be had."

"Is there a pattern to the thefts?" I asked. "Every other night? Only between certain hours?"

Rochester stroked his beard. "None that I'm aware of. Nina caught a glimpse of the culprit one time. Now I think about it, she said there was a strange mark on the thief's forehead, which neither of you has."

I noticed the loaves of bread on the shelf just past his arm and my stomach rumbled. To his credit, Rochester didn't remark on the sound. He simply reached for the loaf of bread.

"Why don't we break bread while we talk? I've got a small table set up behind the counter where I take my breaks."

Rochester started toward the back of the store, picking up a stick of butter along the way. "I promise to fix you a proper meal later, but I won't make it through this conversation without eating."

There was only one chair, so we stood around the table. Rochester smeared butter on multiple slices and set them on a plate in the middle. I was grateful for his kindness.

"Did Nina describe the mark on the thief's forehead?" I asked, chewing hungrily.

"Looked like an eye. She didn't have a weapon that Nina could see. Didn't use magic neither."

"Human," Callan and I said in unison.

"Could be a Cyclops worshipper," Callan remarked.

I shook my head. "She had a third eye not a single one."

"Yes, but she didn't *actually* have a third eye. She had one painted on."

I looked at him askance. "Are you aware of any Cyclops worshippers?"

The vampire tossed a piece of bread into his mouth and chewed. "No. Doesn't mean they don't exist though. People will worship anything under the right conditions. Look at celebrity culture before the Eternal Night."

I couldn't argue with his assessment.

"She might be one of the Mierce," I ventured. The Mierce were humans that dwelled in the borderlands in an effort to avoid vampire rule. It made sense that they might steal from small villages—they wanted to escape detection which meant avoiding towns or cities where a vampire presence was more likely.

Callan chuckled. "The Mierce? They're nothing more than a bedtime story like fairies or elves."

Rochester blew a raspberry, spreading crumbs across the

table. He wiped them away with a nonchalant sweep of his sleeve. "You think they're a fairytale, do you?"

Callan sat straighter and met the older man's gaze. "Of course. My mother read me dozens of stories about them when I was a child. They're nothing more than imaginative adventure stories."

My head swiveled toward him at the rare insight into the vampire's childhood.

"I can assure you the Mierce are very real." Rochester bit into a slice of bread like a dog attacking a bone.

"Have you had experiences with them?" I asked.

"Not directly. Seemed more likely to be strangers passing through like yourselves."

Callan parted the crust from the bread. "And where would someone simply passing through manage to store a broken carriage?"

"There are all manner of hiding spots in these parts. Crags. Woods. Hills. We have it all."

This part of the country was dramatic and beautiful, I'd give him that.

"Do you think the Mierce are dangerous?" I asked.

"I never got that impression. They stick to themselves. People I know have only crossed paths with them when they ventured too close to the borderlands, which don't happen very often."

"You haven't convinced me," Callan said. "Substitute the Mierce for fairies and elves and it's the same story."

Rochester dusted the crumbs from his beard. "I agree that fairies and elves don't walk among us anymore, but they were once as real as you and me."

Callan leaned his back against the counter. "If that were true, then why wouldn't they be here now? Surely the

Eternal Night would've allowed them to emerge from the shadows as well."

Rochester puffed out his ruddy cheeks. "What kind of education do you get up there in the north? They lived centuries ago alongside witches and vampires and werewolves, but their magic was diluted over time until it was too weak to survive. More and more their kind married and procreated with humans until there was nothing left of them but their stories."

"And how do you know all this?" Callan asked, his voice like velvet.

"I've got fairy blood on my mother's side," he said. "Can't do any magic, of course, but we can trace our lineage back to when every hillock in these parts housed a fairy family."

Callan smirked, clearly amused by the story.

Rochester noticed, too, because he said, "Before the Eternal Night, if anyone had told people that vampires and witches were real, they would've smirked too. If they could be wrong then, why can't we be wrong now?"

Callan's smirk faded.

I considered mentioning my run-in with the Korriganes, nine Celtic fairies with deadly breath that used the air around them to change shape, but now didn't seem like the right time.

"I'll see if I can find your thief," I said.

Callan started to choke and I gave his back a powerful whack.

"That's excellent news. Thank you kindly." Rochester hiked up his trousers. "If you'll pardon me, I need to relieve myself. My bladder's like a bucket with a hole in it these days."

Once he was out of earshot, Callan turned his attention to me. "You can't be serious."

"Why not? These people need help. What kind of knight would I be if I abandoned them in their hour of need?"

"Hour of need?" he scoffed. "Don't you think that's a bit of an exaggeration."

"I know it's hard for you to imagine given your privileged lifestyle, but people in this village will likely die within the next six months if we don't recover their livestock."

The vampire's gaze drifted to the half-eaten loaf of bread. "Do you have time to spare for this? What about the berserkers?"

"I can handle both." The villagers' need was more pressing. They relied on each other for sustenance and the livestock took time to grow and fatten. If the thief continued to operate, the entire village would starve.

"I certainly wasn't expecting all this when I followed you to Paddington."

"Serves you right."

Rochester returned to the table. "I'll have my wife, Mary, fix you a meal before you start your search."

"Could you also give us directions to Bramblemoor?" I asked. "We were told she might have room for us to stay the night."

Rochester tugged his beard. "Don't think she will. I hear her place is full of traveling musicians this week."

I cut a glance at Callan. "We can drive to Exeter tonight and find a place there."

"Nonsense," Rochester interrupted. "I'll ask Nina to make up the beds at her place. Much better than anything Exeter has to offer. I'd offer you our spare room, but we've got someone staying there."

"A lodger?" I asked.

Rochester averted his gaze. "Not exactly. Just someone in need of a place to recuperate. Kind of a strange story."

I cut a quick glance at Callan. "Is your guest a werewolf by any chance?"

Rochester's eyelashes fluttered with surprise. "What makes you ask that?"

I felt my excitement rise. "Would it be possible for me to speak with him?"

Rochester looked from me to Callan. "I don't know. What is it you want to ask him?"

"It's about the storm," I said. "Is he coherent?"

"His speech is slower, but otherwise, sure."

I persuaded Rochester to let us speak to him while supper was being prepared.

"See?" I told Callan on our way to Rochester's house. "Not such a detour after all, is it?"

"We're not far from where the rivers converge. It makes sense that one or two would've made it as far as Mirth."

Mary greeted us at the front door. She was a slender woman with surprisingly muscular arms, no doubt due to the physical labor she regularly performed. It couldn't be easy for her.

She gave us each a hard look. "My husband says you're going to find our thief. Good." She turned swiftly. "This way. I'll take you to Mulberry."

"That's his name?" I asked.

"That's what we call him. Found him near death by a mulberry bush. Says he doesn't have a name." She opened a door at the back of the house. "Mulberry, you have visitors." She ushered us in and closed the door behind us, leaving us alone with the mysterious guest.

He was tucked under a white sheet in a twin bed. His hair was long and shaggy and someone had attempted to shave his face but appeared to give up partway. His brown eyes regarded us warily.

Instinctively I lowered myself to a chair so as not to tower over him. "My name is London and this is Mr. Lincoln."

Callan kept his distance, leaning against the door with his arms folded. He seemed uncertain.

The man grunted.

"Can you talk?" I asked.

He nodded. "They call me Mulberry."

"But you don't know your name?"

"Never had one," he said, choosing each word with care.

I decided to cut to the chase. "Is it because you've spent your life in wolf form until recently?"

His gaze darted to Callan before returning to me.

"It's okay," I assured him. "We're not here to hurt you. We only want to understand what happened."

"Don't know," he said. "There was a storm. We sought shelter. Afterward we headed for our usual spot near the rivers, but..." He trailed off.

"You were in wolf form during the storm?" I asked.

He nodded.

"And how long afterward?" Callan prompted.

"Not sure. Couple days, I think. Storm caught us by surprise. We were farther from home than we would've liked. I didn't make it. Woke up here instead."

"Are you certain?" The timing seemed critical.

He nodded again.

"Do you happen to recall seeing people with marks on their foreheads?"

His brow creased. "Marks?"

"The image of an eye." I pointed to my forehead. "Here."

"The moors. The place where the ponies gather."

"Thank you. That's helpful."

"What about the rest of you?" Callan asked. "Where are they now?"

Mulberry sank deeper beneath the sheet, the weight of his sadness seemed to drag him down. "Don't know."

"Have you shifted back to wolf form since you discovered your human form?" I asked.

Mulberry blinked at me, uncertain.

I resumed a standing position. "Give it a try when you feel up to it. I know it might seem scary, but you should be able to control the transformations now." If Mulberry was more comfortable living his life as a wolf, there was nothing to stop him. "It was nice to meet you. Good luck with everything."

I started toward the door.

"Full moon tonight," he said.

I glanced over my shoulder at him. "Are you sure?"

He closed his eyes. "A wolf always knows."

10

The air was thick with fog as we made our way across the moors in the jeep. We rode with the lights on low so as not to draw attention, although there was nothing we could do about the sound of the motor.

"As if we needed the world to be even darker," I muttered.

Callan grinned at me. "What's the matter, brave knight? Afraid of the dark?"

"Look at this place. I bet it's crawling with monsters."

"You seem to forget you travel with the most dangerous monster of all." His fangs glimmered in the dim light.

I hadn't forgotten. Not even for a second.

"How is it that Mulberry can speak with a human tongue?" Callan asked.

"No idea. I imagine there's a lot about this world we don't understand." The stones. The berserkers. Traveling alone with a deadly vampire. As far as I was concerned, my whole reality was being called into question.

"You really think he'll be able to shift back?" Callan asked.

"If my theory is correct, yes."

"Your theory being that a stone like the two in our possession can influence shapeshifters?"

I nodded.

"Will you be disappointed if you're wrong?"

My gaze flicked to him. "What do you mean?"

"I feel like part of you wants to point to some external reason for bad behavior so you can absolve them of wrongdoing. Maybe there are simply crazed wolves in the world who act like primitive animals and sometimes those animals attack people."

"Like there are vampires who prey on the weak and vulnerable instead of going through the proper channels?"

He frowned. "Why do I get the sense there's a story there?"

I told him about the vampire den in Mayfair and what happened to Judd's family.

Callan was silent for a prolonged moment. "I'll look into it for you when we return to the city."

I looked at him askance. "Why would you do that?"

"Because you're right. Like many things, it shouldn't have happened. I'll do my part to set matters right."

This vampire seemed very different from the Prince Callan who strutted around the city. I took a chance and raised an uncomfortable subject.

"Is this because of what happened in Birmingham?"

His fingers tightened on the wheel. "No one has ever spoken to me about that day. Not even the king himself."

"Want to talk about it?" The moment felt strangely intimate.

"I don't remember much, to be honest, although I wish I could remember every detail."

A sharp intake of breath followed his admission and he shot a quick glance at me.

"Oh, no. Not to relish it. To own it. I owe it to those people to remember what happened. What I did."

"Did you know what you were doing?"

He kept his eyes on the road. "Of course. I was twelve. Old enough to know." He stopped before he added 'better.'

"It's not unusual for a boy to strive to please his father, especially a father who's also his king." I was treading on dangerous ground but something spurred me on.

"I knew what I was doing. I was a powerful vampire even at that age and I was eager to prove it. I would have left a trail of corpses all the way to the city if the war hadn't ended first. I was angry when I was made part of the treaty and I was even angrier when Dale died."

"That was your cousin's name?"

He nodded. "I didn't have any siblings. Dale was the closest thing I had until House Lewis took me in."

"I can understand why you were angry." His father treated him like property to be discarded at will. I had to wonder about the first twelve years of his life.

"Doesn't make it right, but I can't undo it."

After that exchange, a wall dropped down between us. I felt the change in the air and noticed the tension in his body. Pushing the Demon of House Duncan too far seemed like a very bad idea.

"See any ponies yet?" I asked, eager to change the subject.

He peered through the windshield. "Not yet. You're sure this is the right direction?"

I shrugged. "I asked Rochester where the ponies gather on the moors and this is the way he sent us." I lowered my window and hung my head outside. "There's nowhere to hide livestock and a carriage out here."

"What do you mean? You could hide them two meters from us in this fog and we wouldn't spot them." Callan's nostrils flared. "Do you smell that?"

I lowered my window further and sniffed the air. A metallic scent wafted past us as the air stirred. Blood.

"No. What is it?" I couldn't let him know that my ability to scent blood rivaled his own. That fact would raise questions I couldn't answer without risking my life.

"It isn't human."

He pulled off the road and slowed the jeep to a stop. "We should travel on foot from here."

"Feel free to stay here and wait. Your brother isn't interested in whether a Devonshire village gets its livestock back."

His face registered mild surprise. "You'd go alone? You have no idea what you're walking into."

I strapped my axe to my back and adjusted my daggers. "I never do. Such is the life of a knight."

He locked the doors and stuffed the keys in his pocket. "I'm coming with you."

"Suit yourself." Was it possible to feel both pleased and terrified? Callan had a way of pressing both of those buttons.

We traipsed across the moors bathed in fog and darkness. I heard the grunts of pigs in the distance. We were on the right track.

We emerged from the fog and I spotted a cow as well as the carriage on the horizon. The animal was attached to the carriage. It seemed like any moment Cinderella and her fairy godmother would appear to turn it into a stallion and a golden carriage. It was then I noticed the people.

"What's going on?" Callan whispered.

We crouched low to the ground.

"Some kind of ritual." Who knew which gods the Mierce worshipped? Maybe this was their annual prayer for a bountiful harvest.

A young woman moved through the small crowd to stand in the center of a ring of rocks. Even in the darkness, I could see the tattoo of the eye on her forehead. A human skull rested on her head like a crown of bones.

"Our thief?" Callan asked in a low voice.

I nodded. What was she doing? Her dress was surprisingly fancy for a woman in the middle of nowhere surrounded by stolen pigs.

But where was the blood we smelled? They'd likely slaughtered one of the pigs to kick off the ritual.

A flicker of reddish-orange light caught my eye. A man in a golden cloak walked toward the circle carrying a flaming torch. The crowd parted as he made his way to the young woman in the center. He said a few words, but I couldn't decipher them. The people bowed their heads in response.

The cloaked man lowered the torch to the skull on her head so that it was wreathed in flames and stepped away. For a shining moment I was transfixed by the striking vision —until I realized the flames weren't stopping at the skull. They quickly spread to her hair and clothes.

This wasn't just a ritual.

This was a sacrifice.

"Holy hellfire," Callan breathed.

I turned myself invisible and tore across the empty space between us. I cut straight through the throng of bodies and tackled the young woman to the ground, rolling her back and forth on the earth to smother the flames. Her skin and dress were black with smoke and ash, but she was alive. I returned to my visible form and drew a deep, cleansing breath.

Glaring at me, she slapped both hands on my chest and shoved me. "Do you have any idea what you've done?"

I climbed to my feet. "It's called saving you. You're welcome."

She snatched the skull from the ground where it had fallen and stuffed it back on her head. "I volunteered. This was a great honor."

I pressed my lips together in frustration. What was it with people and noble sacrifices?

I suddenly became aware that I was surrounded by people with burning torches—people who appeared unhappy to see me.

"I don't want to hurt you," I said.

The young woman's face hardened. "And I was thinking how I'd very much like to hurt *you* right now."

The man in the golden cloak stepped closer to me. His eyes glinted with buried rage. "You have no idea what you've done."

It only took a moment to connect with my magic. I felt the familiar sensation of fitting a key into a lock and twisting until I felt that satisfying click. I let it rise to the surface but held it at bay, waiting to see whether it was necessary.

The man studied my face. "She has power," he announced, keeping his gaze on me. "Perhaps this is fortuitous." He removed the skull from the young woman's head and placed it on mine.

Callan chose this moment to make his presence known. "Leave her be!" The vampire pushed his way through the crowd with his fangs on display. The sight of them sent a shiver spiraling through me.

"Callan, don't." The last thing I wanted was for him to launch himself into a violent frenzy.

The people raised their torches as though preparing to strike the vampire. I jumped in front of him and spread my arms wide.

"Trust me," I warned. "You don't want to do that. He's more powerful than he looks."

Callan looked at me with a pinched expression. "Hey!"

"We do not acknowledge vampire rule," the cloaked man said. Murmurs of assent followed his declaration.

Callan retracted his fangs. "I'm not here to rule you."

"You stole from the village of Mirth," I said. I waved a hand toward the livestock and carriage. "You've taken food they desperately need."

"For a greater purpose," the cloaked man said.

I removed the skull from my head. "And what purpose is that?"

"Ushas," the young woman replied. "We're attempting to revive her through me."

Callan shot me a quizzical look. "You're the walking library. Who's Ushas?"

Memories clicked into place as I remembered a story my mother told me.

"Goddess of the dawn," I said. Like other groups I'd encountered, the Mierce were using an ancient ritual to try to bring back the sun. This time it was through channeling the goddess of the dawn.

The vampire required no further explanation.

"I can't let you do this," I said. "It won't work and you'll have murdered one of your own for nothing." Another life wasted.

The cloaked man snatched the skull from my hands. "You know nothing."

"I know enough to know this isn't the way."

The man held the skull to his chest and withdrew from the crowd. "Kill them."

The metal points of spears sliced through the darkness.

I tipped back my head and groaned in exasperation. "Please don't. We're trying so hard to play nice."

The circle tightened around us. I reached out with my mind to see if I could enlist help. The cow and pigs were useless.

I pressed outward and brushed against a collection of minds. The ponies. Individually a pony wasn't much of a threat. A string of ponies, however...

I latched on to their minds and summoned them toward us. A tip of metal pierced the skin of my arm as the Mierce began their attack.

I released my axe and swung.

Out of the corner of my eye, I saw Callan hook an arm around one of their necks and use him as a human shield.

I returned my focus to the people around me. Despite their efforts to kill me, I didn't want to hurt them if I could avoid it. I only wanted to return what was taken from Mirth.

I used the blunt end of my axe to subdue my attackers. A few well-placed hits and they were on the ground, unconscious.

But they kept coming.

Thunder rolled toward us and the ground trembled beneath our feet.

Finally.

I squinted through the darkness as the ponies arrived on the moor.

Not ponies.

Wild stallions.

They stampeded toward us, forcing the crowd to

disperse. I dodged a spear as well as the pounding hooves. A few people failed to move in time and succumbed to the herd.

I whistled to get their attention. Twelve stallions came to a halt on my command.

The Mierce gaped at me.

"What power is this?" the cloaked man demanded.

"One you can only dream of," I said.

His hand thrust forward and grabbed me by the throat. "Your sacrifice will bring Ushas to us."

Blood spurted on my face and the man's arm was on the ground, still wrapped in the sleeve of the golden cloak. The man screamed and fled.

Callan stood beside me and roared at the remaining Mierce. They huddled together and backed away from us.

"You will leave the village of Mirth in peace," he said. "And you will forget this absurd ritual."

He turned and stalked toward the jeep. I glanced at the arm on the ground, now resting in a pool of blood.

I hurried after Callan. "How are we going to get the livestock and the carriage back to Mirth?"

"You've got that neat animal trick. Tell them to follow us until we reach the village. Leave the carriage. They said it was no use to them anyway."

I released my hold on the stallions and connected with the livestock to give them instructions. Although I couldn't have a telepathic conversation, they'd get the gist of it. The pigs were smarter than the cow, but they were both easy to manipulate.

We drove without speaking until we reached the outskirts of Mirth.

Callan was first to break the silence. "I won't apologize for the arm."

"I won't ask you to."

He arched an eyebrow but said nothing.

"I get it. You were protecting me."

"You gave them plenty of chances to be reasonable."

"I did." I paused. "You didn't feed on his blood."

He looked at me askance. "Would you rather I did?"

"No, but I noticed that before. When we fought in the city…I would've expected…" I trailed off, uncertain how to proceed.

His jaw tightened. "I'm not one of your animals, London. I find it best not to make assumptions about a species you're not a member of."

I turned back to the darkness of the window and fell silent. The vampire prince had no idea how wrong he was.

We stayed the night at Nina Stark's house and she was so thrilled by the return of the livestock that she insisted on packing us sandwiches for the road the next morning. I told her I was a vegetarian so she didn't waste their much-needed food on me. I'd been thankful that Mary's earlier stew had been only root vegetables and green beans.

Callan refueled the jeep and we drove to the nearest highway.

"Back to Exeter?" he asked.

I nodded. "We have plenty of time to make the train."

"How are you going to track the object in Britannia City?"

I watched the passing countryside. "Connect the dots of berserkers until it forms a complete picture."

"Sounds reasonable."

We'd almost made it to Exeter when we encountered a roadblock.

I craned my neck for a better view. "What is it? An accident?"

Callan stuck his head out the window. "Looks like some kind of patrol."

"What are they looking for?"

"Not us, I hope."

Our turn arrived and Callan offered the two patrolmen a pleasant smile.

The vampire snapped his fingers. "Out of the vehicle, please."

"What's this about?" Callan asked.

"Security check on account of the gala tonight at the castle," the shorter vampire said. "We need to see your papers."

Callan and I exited the jeep and I walked around the front to stand beside him.

The taller vampire's eyes widened as he got a closer look at Callan. "Glory be. Don't need no papers from him." He lowered himself to one knee and bowed his head. "Forgive me, Your Highness. You must be here for the gala."

The shorter vampire laughed. "Get up, you fool. This isn't a prince of House Peyton."

The genuflecting vampire's hand shot out with preternatural quickness and whacked the back of his friend's knees. The shorter vampire dropped to the ground and yowled.

"What'd you do that for?"

"This is Prince Callan of House Duncan."

The shorter vampire snuck a peak at Callan. "You sure?"

"My sister kept his pictures tacked on her bedroom wall for years. Yeah, I'm sure."

"You may rise," Callan said. "Yes, we're here for the gala.

This is my date, London Hayes. She's a knight from Britannia City."

The shorter vampire laughed uproariously. "A girl knight? That's a tall tale if I ever heard one."

Callan and I exchanged glances.

"If you don't believe me, why don't I show you?" I asked.

Callan placed a hand on my arm. "No need for displays of strength, dearest."

The shorter vampire snorted. "No, I'd like to see her display of strength."

Oh, boy.

The idiot smiled at me. "Let's go, poppet."

Poppet? My mother didn't even call me poppet when I was seven.

I clocked him right in the face and heard the crunch of bone.

"Oops," I said.

The vampire cradled his face to catch the dripping blood. "You broke my nose."

His companion laughed.

Callan clapped my shoulder. "He said he wanted to see."

The injured vampire whimpered. "She didn't count to three. I assumed there'd be an official countdown."

"We'll be on our way now," Callan said.

"No, no. You're to be escorted directly to the castle. King and queen's orders," the taller vampire insisted.

My stomach clenched.

"We're meant to meet a friend at the train station," I said. "That's where we're going now. We'll head to the castle afterward."

"No trains arriving now," the taller one said. "Too early. Come on then. We'll be your official escort." He waved to another patrolman and indicated the jeep. "Hansen will bring your jeep to the castle carpark."

"That's...very kind of you," I said. What else could we do?

The taller vampire gave Callan an admiring glance. "I can't believe the Demon of House Duncan is attending the gala. Wait until I tell my sister. She'll be so jealous." His smile dissolved. "I shouldn't call you that, should I? Apologies, Your Highness."

Callan waved him off. "Water under the bridge."

The patrolmen ferried us into the backseat of a golf cart and drove us across rolling hills until we arrived at the castle entrance. I recognized the building from history books.

Technically a fortified manor house, Peyton Castle was once known as the Manor of Powderham and later Powderham Castle. It was even mentioned in the Domesday Book. Its position on the River Exe and close to the city of Exeter made it an ideal location.

Less than ideal for us, of course. If it had been farther away, we would've made it to the train station without interference.

We exited the golf cart and were escorted to the castle entrance. Two guards flanked the door. The guard on the right took one look at the vampire with the bloody nose and recoiled.

"You all right, Robert?"

"An accident," Robert said.

Callan clapped him on the back. "Poor sod. Wasn't watching where he was going. Ran straight into the side of our jeep."

Robert cast him an aggrieved look. "They're guests for the gala."

The guard on the right brightened. "Good timing. You

can pay your respects to the king and queen. They're holding court right as we speak."

"It's been a long journey," Callan said. "If it's all the same to you, we'd like to be shown to our quarters first. To freshen up before we see anyone."

The guard on the left jammed his staff into the ground. "You can't simply demand to bypass the king and queen."

"I didn't demand." Callan glanced at me, perplexed. "Did I? I mean, I know I have a certain gravitas when I speak…"

I sighed and lightly touched his arm. "Gentlemen, this is Prince Callan of Houses Duncan and Lewis. If I were you, I'd let him do what he wants."

The guard on the left gasped in recognition. "The Highland Reckoning?"

I nudged Callan's arm. "See? You're a celebrity."

The guard on the left fixed him with a deadpan expression. "You still can't go to your quarters. Not until you've paid your respects to the king and queen."

Callan hesitated and I could tell he was mulling over his options, which were basically to pay his respects or start a war between Houses.

Finally he offered an anemic bow. "I'd be happy to pay my respects."

The guard on the left dipped his hand into his pocket and retrieved a pen. "Before you go, would you mind giving me your autograph?"

I stifled a laugh.

Robert and his broken nose remained our escort through the castle.

"This is an amazing place." For a brief moment, I forgot I was surrounded by lethal vampires and let myself enjoy the surroundings. Wood-paneled walls. High ceilings. Portraits.

Long banquet halls. If only my mother were here. She'd be as awestruck as when she entered Buckingham Palace during her brief stint as a teacher.

Robert delivered us to a line of guests outside the State Room where the king and queen were receiving them.

By the time we reached the threshold of the State Room, the dark purple skin of Robert's broken nose had faded to a light pink.

I glimpsed King Marcus and Queen Iris on the dais at the opposite end of the room. With their medium builds, light brown hair, and creamy complexions, they looked similar enough to be siblings. A streak of silver ran through Iris's hair, the sign of a long life. Vampires with full heads of silver hair were rare, but if you saw one, it was best to steer clear. Vampires didn't reach old age by being warm and fuzzy.

Robert strode forward. "Prince Callan of Houses Lewis and Duncan and his companion, London Hayes."

A royal vampire on my arm and my knighthood was apparently forgotten.

The queen and king remained remarkably impassive given the surprise announcement.

"Truly?" the queen asked. Her gaze raked over him. "You have your father's eyes."

Callan bowed. "Forgive the unexpected arrival, Your Majesty."

The king observed him coolly. "What brings you to Devon?"

"And why were we not informed in advance?" the queen added.

"A failure in communication, I'm afraid," Callan said. "My deepest apologies. May I say you have a gorgeous home here."

The queen's lip curled into a slight snarl. "I would have preferred a house that hadn't been occupied by humans for centuries, but I lost that particular battle." A weak sigh escaped her pink lips. "My husband sees it as a triumph. That we've taken what's theirs and made it our own." She rolled her eyes. "We've taken their whole world, darling. Can we not build a house that reflects who we are rather than who we defeated?"

House Lewis had taken a different approach and completely gutted what was once Buckingham Palace. They retained the shell but not much else.

Movement caught my eye and I looked down to see a tortoise crawl across the slabs of stone. I'd never actually seen one in person before.

My delight must've been evident because the king smiled. "Ah, one of our castle pets has come to join us."

A tortoise seemed a strange choice for the ruling vampire family.

"My father prefers stags," Callan said. "We had several that roamed the grounds in Scotland when I was a boy."

The queen watched the tortoise make its way slowly across the floor. "Before the Great Eruption, this castle had a walled garden with a small animal kingdom for visiting children. The only animal to survive and thrive was the tortoise. There are at least a dozen of them roaming about the grounds. I objected to them at first, but I must admit, they won me over in the end."

Callan glanced down to admire the creature. "Slow and steady wins the race, indeed."

I didn't bother to forge a connection with the tortoise. He seemed perfectly content with his situation. Not that I blamed him. If you're going to live a long time in one place, you could do a lot worse than Peyton Castle.

"I heard we've been graced with a special guest." A vampire swept into the hall wearing a pale blue cloak and matching shoes with pointy toes. She was no more than twenty with auburn hair that cascaded past her shoulders and a button nose. The adorable features stopped at her mouth, which was lined with red that accentuated her shining white fangs. It was a mouth designed to inflict pain and cruelty.

Callan immediately lowered his head and I followed suit. "Princess Louise, I presume," he said.

The princess took her place by her father's side and studied the Demon of House Duncan from head to toe. "Father, was this your idea?"

"Certainly not. I didn't know until now."

The princess frowned. "Surely the other Houses wouldn't bypass protocol."

"I can explain, Your Majesty," Callan said.

"I'd love to hear it," the king said.

"I've accompanied my companion, London Hayes of the Knights of Boudica..."

The king's focus turned to me. "Knight? But you're a woman."

The queen patted her husband's arm. "There, there, darling. I know it's a shock to the system, but women are capable of far more than childbirth and domestic duties."

The king clapped a weary hand against his cheek and shook his head. "My wife mocks me."

"We paid a visit to Albemarle to see the earl," Callan continued. "We were en route to the train station to return to Britannia City when we were redirected by members of your team."

"Now that you're here, we insist you stay for the gala this

evening." The queen cast a quick glance at her daughter and I immediately understood.

"An excellent notion," the king chimed in. "I believe there's room for distinguished guests in Courtenay Tower, isn't there?"

"We shall make room," the queen stated.

I swallowed hard. An entire castle teeming with vampires?

"We appreciate the gesture..." Callan began, but the queen cut him off.

"Nonsense. There will be five hundred guests in attendance. Imagine how excited they'll be to discover your presence among them. Tonight you shall be the jewel in *our* crown." She turned to the princess. "Louise, speak to Esmerelda about a dress for our knight." The queen raised her thinly drawn eyebrows at me. "Unless you'd prefer decorative armor?"

"A dress would be fine," I said. "Thank you for your generosity."

"Any friend of House Duncan is a friend of ours," the queen said.

"House Lewis," Callan reminded her.

The queen's smile didn't quite reach her eyes. "Yes, of course. Naturally our esteemed neighbor House Lewis."

The king whistled through his fangs, creating a shrill sound that jolted me. "Edwards, please deliver our guests safely to Courtenay Tower." He looked back at us. "The staff there will attend to you."

I wasn't thrilled by the prospect of more time among vampires, but I didn't see a way to object without drawing their ire. I'd be careful, keep my head down, and escape to the train station in the morning.

Edwards escorted us to another golf cart that delivered

us across the grounds to the riverbank where Courtenay Tower was located. I'd originally thought the queen meant one of the six towers connected to the castle. This separate accommodation was a relief. Maybe I could hide in here all night and meet Callan at the train station tomorrow.

"I'm sorry about this," Callan said, once we arrived inside the tower. "If it weren't for my insistence on accompanying you, we wouldn't be here."

Edwards opened one door. "Your Highness." He continued along the corridor and opened a second door. "Miss."

I entered the round room with its large canopy bed and heavy furniture. The bedroom was bigger than my entire flat.

"Adjoining rooms," I murmured, noting the door that connected Callan's to mine.

On cue, the door flew open and Callan appeared. "A convenient feature."

I stared at him. "Convenient for what?"

"Esmerelda will be with you shortly." Edwards bowed and left us alone.

I gave voice to my thoughts. "Maybe I should stay here and let you go alone."

"And miss a House gala?"

"I'm not really a gala kind of girl."

His penetrating gaze sent tiny shockwaves throughout my body. "I'm afraid staying here isn't an option."

"Why not?"

"It would be taken as an insult. Battles were fought over less."

"Then maybe vampires need to reexamine their priorities."

His green eyes flashed with indignation. "You have no idea how House politics work."

Nor did I want to.

"You will attend the gala on my arm."

My eyebrows rose. "Is that a royal decree?"

"Call it whatever you like. Just be ready when I call for you." He retreated into his room and shut the door between us.

Be ready when he called for me? Was I a dog now?

I spun on my heel and disappeared into the bathroom where I released a bit of magic.

There. Much better.

I washed my face, untangled the knots from my hair, and waited for Esmerelda to arrive.

If I was about to enter the belly of the beast, I might as well look good doing it.

11

The queen wasn't exaggerating about the number of guests at the gala. My skin burned in response and my supernatural defenses were going haywire in an effort to alert me to all the potential threats. At least my magic was behaving. I was a normal shade of beige with nary a silver fleck in sight. Now I just had to stay that way for the duration of the gala.

Callan and I entered through the State Room to be welcomed by the royal family and continued to the ballroom. I caught Callan looking at me for what seemed like the fiftieth time and I finally broke my silence.

"Is there something on my face?" Aside from makeup, of course. I touched the corner of my mouth to check whether the lipstick had smudged. If Kami could see me now, she'd die laughing.

The prince seemed taken aback by the question. "No, you look...exquisite."

I glanced down at the dress I'd been loaned. The sapphire fabric complemented my coloring and the A-line skirt emphasized my small waist and had the added bonus of making it easy to move in.

"Try not to look so surprised."

He said nothing and turned his attention to the ballroom where the gala was already underway. Vampires danced in pairs and even threesomes, although the latter moved so awkwardly I didn't see why they bothered. There was no fun in constantly bumping elbows and tripping over each other's feet.

I felt the gaze of dozens of vampires as word spread of the prince's arrival and it didn't take long for Princess Louise to find us.

"Prince Callan, how splendid you look." She wrinkled her nose at me. "You, too, of course, lady knight."

"Her name is London," Callan corrected her.

She gave him a coy smile. "Did you know we were once discussed as a match? To join our Houses."

Callan maintained an air of indifference. "I wasn't aware."

She plucked two flutes of blood from a passing server and handed one to Callan. The smell was nauseating.

"I don't know what became of it," Louise continued. "Perhaps we should inquire." She flashed an engaging smile that showed her fangs.

Callan took the flirtation in stride. "With my reputation, I would be a heavy burden for any woman. You'd be much better off with someone like my brother, Maeron."

"But my father has no interest in a match with House Lewis. He is, however, quite interested in a union with House Duncan." She lowered her lashes in a coquettish fashion. "Prudent marriages have been a staple of our survival, you see."

My gaze darted to Callan, who remained impassive. "A

prudent marriage to the Highland Reckoning seems counterintuitive to me," he replied.

"Why are you traveling together outside of House Lewis territory?" She tipped back the flute and emptied the glass of its contents.

"An assignment that required royal supervision." Callan tapped the outside of his flute, the contents untouched.

The princess regarded me. "A knight who requires a protector? Why bother calling yourself a knight at all?"

"He's not..." I started, but Callan interrupted.

"We knew an encounter with the Mierce was likely given our destination and my House hoped to avoid a diplomatic incident. King Casek decided it best to send an emissary along with his best knight."

It wasn't even a good lie, but the princess seemed to swallow it whole.

"Ugh, the Mierce. They've troubled our House for quite some time. I can't travel to the coast without soldiers because of them. Father thinks it's too risky. If it were up to me, I'd send the army after them. Set their heads on spikes to warn others what happens to traitors."

"They're more misguided than harmful," Callan said. "I wouldn't waste your resources on them."

The princess tugged at the collar of his shirt in a playful fashion. "Perhaps you wish to lull us into a false sense of security. After all, House Lewis stands to benefit if our House is weakened by a Mierce uprising."

"If they're a significant threat to your House, then they're a threat to ours," Callan pointed out.

She removed the flute from his hand and drank it, keeping her eyes glued to him the whole time.

"Dance with me," she said.

"Of course, Your Highness." Without so much as a

glance at me, he took her by the hand and escorted her to the dance floor.

At least they didn't try to make it a threesome.

I watched them for a brief moment before seeking refuge. What did I care that he'd placed his hand on the small of her back? Those two were made for each other. Princess Louise was hard and cruel and Prince Callan was terrifying. I'd be lucky to be rid of him soon.

I ambled through the cavernous rooms of the castle until a pleasant scent permeated my nostrils.

Citrus?

I followed the trail until I reached the open doorway to a courtyard. I stood on the threshold and blinked in surprise. The courtyard was lined with trees bearing fruit. I'd never seen so much in one place, not even at the market. I walked to the nearest tree to examine the oblong green fruit.

"Lime trees," a voice said. "Her Majesty planted them when they first took over the castle."

I turned to see a girl in a white satin dress. She couldn't have been a day older than twelve. "You know the history?"

"My mum told me. She works here. She oversees the magic users who keep the trees on the castle grounds alive."

"Why lime trees?" I knew the answer, but I wondered whether she did.

The girl squared her shoulders. "Because they're impressive. No other House in the country grows lime trees as far as I know."

"That's certainly one reason." The other reason was that lime trees, along with linden trees, were believed to inspire truthfulness. I'd bet good money that if the king or queen wanted information from staff, they were interviewed in this very courtyard. Glancing around to make certain I wasn't observed, I plucked a lime from the nearest branch and stuffed the small object into the bodice of my gown. No one would search for it there and they'd lose a hand if they tried. I held a finger over my lips and smiled at the little girl. It would be our secret.

Callan appeared at the opposite end of the courtyard and the girl's eyes grew as large as the limes. "Is it true?" she whispered.

"Is what true?" I asked.

"Is he truly…You know?" Her eyes stayed pinned to the prince.

"He really is."

She looked at me agape. "And you travel with him?"

"We work together."

"He doesn't frighten you?"

All vampires frightened me, but I pushed back against the influence of the lime trees and kept my mouth shut.

"I'm a knight. It takes more than fangs to frighten me. How about you? You're a young witch in a castle full of vampires. Doesn't that frighten you?"

She lowered her gaze. "Every day."

I crouched down and placed a reassuring hand on her shoulder. "I think you're very brave and the world needs brave women. Practice your magic as much as they'll allow it. It's your best weapon."

"And then I can become a knight like you?"

I looked into her innocent eyes. "Maybe when you're older, the world will no longer need knights."

Callan reached us and the girl curtsied before racing back inside.

"I was wondering where you'd wandered off to," he said. "Made a friend, did you?"

I returned to a standing position. "Wherever I go. How was your dance?"

"Adequate. Princess Louise doesn't suffer from a lack of confidence, I'll say that much." His gaze swept the courtyard. "I've never seen trees like these before. They smell wonderful."

"They do."

Music drifted into the courtyard.

Callan held out a hand. "I believe you owe me a dance."

"Do I?"

"Why not? Away from prying eyes. It would be a nice change."

I eased into his arms. I felt strangely comfortable and was acutely aware of the beating of my heart.

"Why do you think House Peyton would prefer a match with House Duncan when Lewis is their neighbor?"

He clasped my hand in his and we swayed as one. "Are you referring to what Louise said? I wouldn't give it another thought. A manipulation tactic. Nothing more. She wants me to feel more special than Maeron."

"Did it work?"

He grinned. "Does it matter?"

"Learn anything useful about stones or berserkers?"

Callan leaned back and looked me in the eye. "All work and no play makes London a very dull knight."

"Some of us will die without work."

"And many of you die during work." He scowled. "I don't like it."

"What?"

He tightened his hold on my waist. "The thought of you dying."

Well, that was not the response I expected. Then I remembered the lime trees and it occurred to me that a courtyard of lime trees was the last place someone with secrets like mine should be.

I cleared my throat. "We should return to the ballroom before we're missed."

He leaned closer. "What's the rush?" His breath was warm on my ear and an involuntary shiver escaped me. Callan seemed to misinterpret my reaction because he said, "You have no reason to fear me. I would never hurt you."

I had to get out of the courtyard before I said something I'd regret. I disentangled myself and hurried inside without another word.

The gala was still going strong and I was captivated by the number of couples dancing. Two men swirled past me and I jumped back to avoid a collision.

Callan was beside me again. His handsome features were etched with concern. "Did I say something to upset you?"

"No." I cast a wary glance in the direction of the courtyard. We had to be away from its sphere of influence now. "I'm sorry. I'm tired from the journey and all the excitement."

His mouth twitched. "Liar."

"I don't look tired to you?"

"I'm not sure. It's hard to see past all that beauty."

I frowned. Maybe the effect of the lime trees extended farther than I thought.

He edged closer so that the sides of our hands were touching. "Would it be so shocking to learn that I'm attracted to you?"

My breath caught in my throat.

"Callan, there you are," Louise's voice interjected. "Father and Mother are here now and they'd like to see us dance." She eyed him like he was raw meat and she was a starving lioness.

"Did they miss it the first three times?"

Her smile evaporated. "You would decline the invitation of your host? What would Queen Imogen say about your manners?" Clucking her tongue, she extended a hand. "Come now. Don't humiliate me in front of our guests. You're the talk of the gala."

His eyes locked on mine as though requesting my approval. It was an unexpected gesture.

"Enjoy yourselves," I said. "I'm heading back to the tower. I'll see you in the morning, Your Highness."

Callan fixed me with those piercing green eyes. "Allow me to accompany you."

I held up a hand to keep him at bay. "No, you stay. Enjoy the spotlight." I noticed dozens of young women clamoring for his attention aside from the princess. I couldn't decide whether they were sizing him up for a husband or sizing me up for a late night snack. Possibly both.

Princess Louise dragged him away by the hand and he disappeared into the crowd without another word.

I hurried from the castle, relieved to put distance between myself and the five hundred vampires at the gala. A quick glance at the silver glow of my hands and I knew I'd waited too long. The moment I was alone in my room, I needed to release a little magic.

I crossed the grounds toward the tower, cutting through the mist that rose from the earth. I glanced over my shoulder at the castle in the distance. Between the mist and the candlelight emanating from the windows, the castle appeared dreamlike, as though it existed between two realities. My head felt much the same. The evening with Callan had thrown me off-kilter and I was relieved that we'd be on the train back to the city tomorrow. Back to the real world where I wore magical armor and didn't dance with vampires in a courtyard of lime trees. The faster I put physical distance between us, the faster I could recover my senses and sensibilities.

I arrived at the tower and opened the rounded wooden door. No guards, thank the gods. I wanted nothing more than to go straight to my room and fall asleep. My body felt heavy with need—for rest. Only for rest. I shook all thoughts of the prince from my mind. It was the strangeness of the trip messing with my emotions. It had to be. I never should've agreed to let him accompany me, not that I'd had much choice. He was a vampire prince and I was…not.

I entered my room and came to a halt. Icy fingernails dragged down my spine and my body shifted to high alert.

Someone was in the room.

A shadow lunged at me and I formed an X with my arms to block my assailant. Sharp nails scraped down my skin and drew blood. A second silhouette sprang from the shadows. I didn't have time to reach for the dagger I had hidden beneath my dress. I did the only thing available to me.

I connected to my magic.

I looked at the candlelight flickering on the bedside table and expanded the flame. Light revealed two vampires dressed in green and white—the colors of House Peyton.

I coaxed the fire toward me while also trying to keep my assailants at bay.

"You like fire so much," the thinner vampire said. "Let's see how it looks on you." He snatched the candlestick from the bedside table and tossed it at me.

I stopped the flames in midair and forced them back toward the vampires. Fire thinned and stretched across the room until it encircled the vampires. They were too dumbfounded to continue their attack and retreated from the flames until their backs were touching.

"What kind of witch are you?" the more muscular

vampire asked. His face looked as though it had been used as a punching bag one too many times.

"I'm asking the questions in this room." I sauntered closer to them, thickening the lasso of flames. "Why are you here?"

"To kill you," the second vampire said. "Why else?"

"Why?" I pressed. "Did someone send you?"

The vampires clamped their mouths closed. I concentrated, tightening the fiery circle around them so that the flames licked their skin.

"Who sent you to kill me?"

They raised their chins in defiance. It seemed they were willing to die for their cause. I'd have to find another way to get the truth out of them.

The truth.

I reached into the bodice of my dress and retrieved the lime I'd hidden there. I reached straight through the flames and shoved the fruit into the muscular vampire's mouth. He immediately spat it onto the floor. Thankfully he didn't need to eat it in order for it to work.

"Who sent you?" I demanded again.

"The princess." His eyes bulged as he realized he'd given up the information.

"Which one?" As far as I knew, there was only one at the gala, but I needed to be sure.

"Louise," he said.

Princess Louise was more jealous than I realized. "You've got to be kidding me," I muttered. She'd hired these goons to get rid of me because she had a crush on Callan? Was she out of her royal mind? I wasn't even a vampire. How much of an obstacle could I be to her marriage plans?

"What reason did she give?" I asked.

"She doesn't need a reason," the thinner vampire said. "She's the heir to House Peyton. We do as she tells us."

A spoiled and calculating heir, just what the realm needed.

My pulse quickened at a knock on the door.

Before I could answer, the door cracked open and Callan's face appeared. He took one look at the two vampires wreathed in flame and stepped inside, closing the door behind him.

"So this is why you left in such a hurry. A private party." He folded his arms. "Really, London. I'm hurt you didn't invite me."

I glowered at him. "They were waiting for me when I came back to the room and attacked me. They work for your little friend."

He cocked an eyebrow. "Which little friend is that?"

"Starts with Princess and ends with Louise."

He whistled. "You're joking."

"I wish."

He started toward the door. "I'll take care of it."

I rushed to block his exit. "No, absolutely not."

He laughed. "You think I'm going to let this go? They could've killed you."

"But they didn't. Listen, you can't say anything." I wasn't Helen of Troy. No one needed to start a war on my account.

Callan looked at my fingers now encircling his wrist and I released him, slightly embarrassed by the outburst. Touching him like that—the gesture was too familiar. Clearly our flirtatious exchange at the gala had been forgotten, or maybe it had never happened at all. Maybe the lime trees emitted more than a citrus scent and a truthful influence. Maybe they were spelled as well.

His gaze flicked to the two vampires. "What do you think

will happen when these guys return to her with their report?"

"She won't try again. We leave in the morning."

"If you believe that, you don't know royal vampires very well." Callan swaggered toward them with an expression that suggested death and dismemberment. I *never* wanted to be on the receiving end of that particular face.

"Do you know who I am?"

The vampires' heads bobbed in unison.

"Good. You will do two things for me," he said in a voice that demanded nothing short of obedience. "One—you will leave here and never show your face to this woman again. Two—you will tell Princess Louise that your target warded the door to her room and you were unable to carry out the plan. Make it clear the target remains ignorant of the princess's order. Understood?"

Both vampires nodded.

"Good. Dismissed."

I released my hold on the flames and they dissipated. The vampires made a beeline for the door.

I waited until they were gone to relax. "What makes you think they'll obey you over the princess?"

His face hardened. "Experience." He surveyed the room. "I'm staying here tonight. No arguments. It's my fault you're in danger in the first place."

I opened my mouth to object and his fingers gently brushed across my lips and nudged them closed.

"I said no arguments," he said, this time with a surprising softness.

"My clothes are in the bathroom. I'll get changed there."

"If you insist."

I narrowed my eyes. "I do." I turned and walked into the

bathroom, shutting the door behind me with extra flair. The sound of his laughter erupted from the bedroom.

I slipped out of the dress and took solace in the fact that Louise hadn't been clever enough to poison it. She was young, though. Give the vampire enough time and she'd become a challenging adversary for anyone. Tomorrow I'd return to Britannia City with no plans to set foot in Devon anytime soon and the princess would soon forget all about me. So would the prince for that matter.

I scrubbed the makeup from my face and brushed my teeth. When I emerged from the bathroom, the prince was standing by the window gazing outward at the thickening mist.

"Will you go straight to pack headquarters from the train tomorrow?" he asked.

"I haven't decided. Depends on whether the return journey is as eventful as our journey to Exeter."

He cracked a smile. "You do seem to have a penchant for trouble."

"I'm a knight. It's part of the package."

He craned his neck to look at me. "You're still every bit as beautiful as you were at the gala."

I glanced at the lime still on the floor where the vampire had spat it out. I shouldn't have stolen one. Whatever spell it had been treated with was still working its magic on Callan.

"I'm going to bed now."

He inclined his head. "It's king-sized."

I made a sad face. "Ah. Too bad you're only a prince."

His fangs gleamed in the candlelight. "You are a mystery, London Hayes. A glorious, alluring mystery."

"And I shall remain so." I ducked past him and slipped onto the bed. "Good-night, Your Royal Flirt. Sleep well."

"Not at all," he assured me. "I'll be too busy watching over you."

I yawned. "I don't need a stalker. Just go to bed. I've taken care of myself this long. I'll make it one night at Peyton Castle."

His gaze traveled down the length of me. "No blanket?"

"I'm not cold." And it would make it easier to defend myself if I had to leap to my feet.

"How can I offer to keep you warm if you aren't cold?"

"Still flirting," I said. I plumped the pillow and turned my head to face the opposite direction.

It was the lime. There was no other explanation.

Except the lime inspired truthfulness, not deceit.

"I'm impressed you managed to subdue them both on your own."

"Years of practice."

He moved to the other side of the room so that I was facing him again. "Show me."

I frowned. "Show you what?"

"How you ensnared them. I'd like to see your moves."

I laughed. "I'm not showing you anything. Good-night, Your Highness."

His mouth split in a grin. "I meant what I said. You look every bit as beautiful now as you did at the gala."

My heart lodged in my throat. I was torn between wanting to maintain physical distance and wanting to press my body against him so tightly that a single thread couldn't slip between us.

"You don't mean any of this. Tomorrow you'll regret it and it'll make the long trip home awkward."

His gaze locked on mine. "I'm many things, London, and not all of them good. But a liar isn't one of them." He extended a hand. "Now show me."

I found myself unable to resist. I slipped out of bed and stood in front of him.

"I used magic," I whispered. He'd already witnessed my use of elemental magic so I wasn't telling him something he didn't know.

He inched closer to me. "What kind of magic?"

"Hot."

He cocked an eyebrow. "Hot magic? Is that like hot yoga?"

"I used the flame from the candle and molded it into a weapon."

He snaked an arm around my waist. "Very hot, indeed."

He dipped his head and his lips found mine.

I'm kissing a vampire.

And not just any vampire—the Demon of House Duncan.

His fingers threaded through my hair as the kiss intensified. My legs turned to liquid and I worried about losing my balance.

This had to be a dream. Any minute I would open my eyes to find Callan on the floor by the bed or back in his own room.

Any minute now.

His lips migrated to my collarbone, spreading a pleasant tingling sensation throughout my body. He scraped his fangs across my skin and my whole body shuddered.

No.

No. No. No.

It didn't matter how attractive I found him. One night with him wasn't worth my life. What if he figured out what I was?

I had to stop before things went too far.

"What was it like for you in Birmingham?" I blurted.

I felt his body tense. "Why would you ask me that now?"

"Because I want to get to know you better."

"You don't want to know that Callan." He leaned his forehead against mine. "It was the worst day of my life."

Relief flooded me. I'd been hoping for an answer in that vein but had no idea whether I'd get it. Now that I had—did it actually change anything? He was still a dangerous vampire and I was still...

"London?"

"Yes?"

"What was the worst day of your life?"

That was easy. "The day my mother died."

"I'm sorry. What happened?"

"She fell ill and never recovered." I'd sat with her until her final moments and watched her slip away. Tears pricked my eyes as the pain rose to the surface, as fresh as the day it happened.

"And your father?" he asked.

"Don't know. Never met him."

He trailed kisses along the curve of my neck. "I barely remember my mother. Imogen is the only mother figure I've ever known and that isn't saying much."

"But you care for her."

"I do, but more as an elder sister than a mother."

"What's your father like?"

"I haven't missed him if that answers your question. Being given as a hostage to House Lewis was probably the best thing that could've happened to me."

Wow. I could only imagine what the Highland King would have to say about that.

"Maybe you wouldn't feel that way if you'd stayed in Scotland."

"Hard to say. I suppose I would've been brainwashed like

everybody else in my father's orbit. My mother was the only one who didn't seem intimidated by him. I have snippets of memories." He paused as though lost in thought. "When I was a boy, he ordered me to kill the son of a rival family. Apparently the family had been gathering power and prestige and my father worried they'd eventually challenge him. When I refused, he tried to beat me into submission. My mother came bursting into the room with her attendants. Each one carried a weapon they'd taken from the armory." He laughed softly. "The predecessors to your Knights of Boudica. My father backed down in a hurry."

"He didn't hold it against your mother?"

His hands squeezed me. "Eventually. He killed her when her presence was no longer required. She'd given him the son he wanted and was of no more use to him when she could no longer conceive."

His response was so painfully matter-of-fact. I thought about Queen Britannia's untimely death. Now didn't seem the right time to raise the subject.

"I'm so sorry, Callan."

He grazed my shoulder again with his fangs. "You called me Callan."

"That's your name."

He kissed me again and I nearly succumbed.

Nearly.

I splayed my hands on his chest. "I think it would be best if you went to your room or neither of us will sleep."

"Who needs sleep?" The enticing curve of his lips tested every ounce of strength I had.

"I do. Tomorrow I have a stone to track in a city full of them."

He cupped his hand under my chin. "Another time then."

Not if I could help it.

The next morning two guards accompanied us to the train station and I noticed they waited until we'd boarded and the train departed the station before they turned to leave. The king and queen had clearly ordered them to wait and confirm we were en route. Trust between Houses was fragile. So much could've gone wrong during our brief visit. We were fortunate to escape unscathed.

I glanced at Callan and my body flooded with heat at the memory of last night.

Well, relatively unscathed.

I'd left the lime behind. Whatever had transpired between us in Devon, I couldn't risk it following us back to the city. Last night I'd nearly risked everything.

I'd never let that happen again.

12

Our return to the city was uneventful. Callan and I managed to get separated by the crowd during the boarding process and we ended up seated in different carriages, which was for the best. Part of me wondered whether it had been deliberate on his part. I told him last night he'd regret it. Knowing him, the prince was too proud to admit I was right.

I went straight to my flat to welcome home the menagerie and check on the elemental stone. All safe and secure and covered in flour.

I released enough magic to ease the pressure that had been building during the train journey. Water magic to bathe the animals. Fire magic to cook a bowl of porridge for me. I preferred when the magic was productive. Waste not, want not, as my mother used to say.

Once our bellies were full, I showered to wash away Callan's scent and the memory of last night, paying extra attention to my face and neck. What if I'd lost control and let him taste me? With his exceptional abilities, there was every chance he could identify my vampire side and figure out what I was.

Never before had I let my guard down the way I had with Callan. Of all the men in the world, why him? Why couldn't I be attracted to someone safe like a dwarf or even a human? But no, I had to have the hots for a royal vampire with a lethal reputation.

I also worried about the information he'd obtained. Maeron had been smart to send Callan as a spy. Now the vampire prince knew everything I did and the royals could continue their hunt for the stone without me. Despite Callan's promise to keep the information between us, there was a chance Maeron would wheedle it out of him. I couldn't let Maeron find the stone first.

I left the flat and took the bus to the Circus to check in with my team. Trio trotted over to greet me. Three noses sniffed me, presumably for evidence of food. The dog would make quite the narcotics tracker. Kami, Stevie, and Neera were the only knights in the office.

"Where's Minka?" I asked.

"Appointment," Stevie said.

Kami looked up from her desk with a smile. "Hopefully a consultation for a personality transplant."

"Hey, I've been dying to know what happened with Charles," I said. "Do I hear wedding bells?"

Kami grimaced. "You hear the sound of a breaking heart."

"Oh, no. What happened?"

"He thinks I work too much. He wants a woman who can dote on him."

That would never be Kami's style. "I'm sorry."

"On the bright side, Neera met someone." Kami tilted her head toward the earth witch.

Neera smiled. Her light brown hair was styled in a tight French braid today. She and Ione were fastidious about keeping their long hair secure so it didn't get in the way during a fight. My hair was too fine and usually ended up falling out of whatever ponytail or braid I'd attempted.

"Her name is Roxanne and she owns a tea room near our new flat."

"Convenient," I said.

"Not if things don't work out, but I'll take my chances. How was your trip?" Neera asked.

I sat behind my desk. "Good. Learned a few things."

The three knights watched me expectantly.

"That's it?" Kami asked, when I failed to offer more. "You traveled out of House Lewis territory. How many of us can claim that?"

"The countryside is pretty." No way was I telling them about the gala or Peyton Castle. It would lead to questions I didn't want to answer.

"Any luck with your case?" Stevie asked.

"Some. What'd I miss here?" I leafed through the papers on my desk. Boring. More boring. Most boring. "Let me guess. You caught another troll hanging around London Bridge."

Kami snorted. "If only. More like another berserker. Took three of us to subdue him."

My chin snapped up. "Where? When?"

"Notting Hill. Freaked out in the middle of the market."

The blades in my mind started whirring. "Did someone alert you or were you already there?"

"Ione, Neera, and I were on Portobello Road hunting for secondhand furniture for their new flat."

"Say antiques," Neera interjected. "It sounds better."

My pulse sped up. "What happened to the werewolf after you subdued him?"

Kami polished her dagger with a compound bar. "Whisked away by his pack like a group of furry ninjas."

The stone or object—whatever it was—was on the move again. But who was moving it and why?

"I need to talk to the werewolf," I said. "Did you catch his name?"

"They called him Rafe," Neera said.

I grabbed my bag that I'd placed on the back of the chair and slung it over my shoulder. "I need to go."

Kami jumped to her feet. "I'll go. I've got nothing on the schedule."

I hesitated.

"Come on," she urged. "I can identify him if the pack won't help you."

"The pack hired me to help them. It stands to reason they'll cooperate."

Kami gave me a pointed look. "You say that as though the pack always acts sensibly and in its own best interest."

I sighed. "Good point."

Kami beamed and tucked her dagger into its sheath. She waited until we were out of the building to interrogate me.

"Tell me about Devon. What'd you learn?"

"I already told you."

She nudged my elbow. "Come on. I know you better than that. You were withholding information. I could tell."

I told her about my stone theory. If nothing else, it would keep her from asking more probing questions.

"I might know someone who can help."

I snorted. "A stone expert?"

"Sort of. We'll drop in after you interrogate Mr. Meltdown."

We took the bus to pack headquarters on Sloane Street and rang the bell at the window marked 'visitors.' Last time we'd been escorted by werewolves and had bypassed the usual protocols.

The window slid open and a set of amber eyes darted from Kami to me. "Yes?"

"We're looking for Rafe," I said. "We understand he was injured in Notting Hill recently."

"Don't know anyone by that name." He started to close the window. Kami's arm shot out to block it.

"Then find someone who does," she snapped.

The werewolf glared at her. "I don't take orders from witches."

"I'm a knight first and foremost. Kamikaze Marwin, Knight of Boudica. You might know me as the Butcher of Britannia City."

I swallowed a surprised laugh. "I'm London Hayes, also a Knight of Boudica. Tell Romeo Rice I'm asking to see Rafe. He'll know why."

"You can start by telling me."

"That's confidential," I replied.

The werewolf's snarl was subtle but audible. "Hold on a second."

He slid the window closed.

"Why would you tell him that's your name?" I whispered.

Kami shrugged. "I figured it was worth a shot. Your boyfriend's nicknames get results."

Good grief. "First, you didn't destroy half of Birmingham. Second, he's not my boyfriend."

Kami gave me a long look. "I would've thought you'd lead with that second one."

"You're exasperating."

To my great relief, the window slid open again. "He's in the infirmary. Come to the door and we'll buzz you in."

A petite werewolf awaited us at the visitor's entrance. Her name tag said 'Victoria.'

"Is Rafe sick?" I asked.

"He's recuperating."

Kami and I followed her along a narrow corridor and down a staircase.

"Seems impractical to have the infirmary be so challenging to get to," Kami commented.

"You can take it up with the architectural firm," Victoria said. "They did their best with what they had to work with. This building dates back to 1889."

"Who authorized the visit?" I asked. There was no way the two werewolves were senior enough to admit us.

"Romeo is meeting you there as soon as he gets out of a meeting," she said.

That figured. I'd have to offer him a heavily edited report on Devon.

Victoria pressed her palm flat on a pad attached to the door and it clicked open.

"High security for a bay of sick wolves," I remarked.

"We don't always utilize it, but as you obviously know, we've had a few pack members go missing recently, so we've bumped up security measures."

"Why would we know?" Kami queried.

Victoria shot us a quizzical look. "They told me you're both knights. Isn't that why you're here?"

"No, we're working on an unrelated matter," I said.

She winced. "Please don't mention I told you. They'll label me a security risk and send me to an outpost. I don't want to uproot my kids."

There was safety in numbers but pack participation definitely had its downsides.

I pretended to zip my lip and followed her inside. The infirmary was larger than I anticipated with a row of windows and partitioned beds. The room reminded me of photographs I'd seen of recuperating soldiers during World War II.

Victoria inclined her head. "Third bed on the left. I'll wait here."

Kami and I walked past two empty beds until we reached the third one. A werewolf in human form was swaddled in white fabric. All I could see was his head. Even his arms were tucked inside the fabric and I realized it was some kind of restraint system. The cloth was probably spelled to keep him contained.

I sat in the chair adjacent to the bed. "Rafe, my name is London Hayes and this is my colleague, Kami Marwin. We're knights and we have permission to talk to you about the incident in Notting Hill."

He continued to stare at the ceiling without comment.

"I'd like you to tell us everything you remember."

Nothing from Rafe.

"I was there," Kami said. "I helped subdue you. I'm sorry, I know it must've been brutal for you."

"We're trying to get information so we can make sure this doesn't happen to another wolf," I added.

"It's a blur," he rasped.

"I'm sure it seems that way," I said, "but if you really think about it, I bet you'll remember something. I'll take any detail no matter how trivial it seems. Where were you standing when you lost control? Next to a food stall? Furniture? Were you speaking to anyone? Were they holding anything?"

He squeezed his eyes closed. "That's a lot of questions."

"You don't need to answer them all," I said. "I was only offering suggestions."

"I was there to buy a shirt. I like graphic tees."

"The kind with funny expressions or featuring a musician?"

"Funny. This one said 'Beware: Beast Inside.' Had paw prints."

"Sounds great. You weren't meeting anyone?"

The shake of his head was almost imperceptible. "No."

"Any chance you noticed a stone? Possibly one with markings on it?"

His eyebrows pinched together. "A stone? Like for sale?"

"Anywhere."

"No."

Romeo appeared outside the partition. "There's my knight in latex armor."

Kami's lip curled in protest. "It isn't latex."

"How's our boy?" Romeo asked. "Looking good, Rafe." He offered two thumbs up.

I joined Romeo outside the partition. "I don't have an official update yet. I only got back to the city today."

Romeo shoved his hands in his trouser pockets. "Can you give me anything?"

I lowered my voice. "We seem to be searching for an object, most likely a stone, that made its way from Albemarle to the city and continues to be on the move." I angled my head toward Rafe. "Last known location was Portobello Road."

He scratched the dark stubble that lined his chin. "A stone."

I told him about the storm, the dilapidated wall, and the

berserkers who reverted to human form for the first time. I kept the part about the other two stones to myself.

"It's a good theory. Do you think whoever took the stone knows what it can do?" His brow furrowed. "And if so, what are their intentions? Why start a fight at a pub and a market?"

"Not sure. Maybe they're testing it to see what it can do. Maybe they have no clue and it's on the move because the thief is preparing to sell it. I cross-checked the list of everyone at The Crown that night with the list of everyone at Albemarle around the time of the storm. No matches."

Romeo nodded absently. "Okay then. Keep digging."

I glanced at the werewolf wrapped in cotton wool. "Rafe seems back to normal. Why is he here?"

"Mainly for his own protection. Before your friends subdued him, he roughed up a couple of vampires during his frenzy, including the son of one that owns the market. We thought it best to keep him hidden until the incident blows over."

"He's restrained," I pointed out.

"Don't want to take any unnecessary chances. Like you said, it's only a theory. For all we know, Rafe can go nuts again any second."

"In that case, you might want to restrain every werewolf in the city until the matter's been resolved."

His face hardened. "Then I guess you'd better get busy."

I glanced over my shoulder at Rafe. The werewolf's eyes remained closed and I watched as his chest rose and fell. *That's right, Rafe. Deep breaths. You're doing fine, buddy.*

"Come on, Kami."

She perked up. "Where are we headed?"

"You said you knew someone."

She smiled. "I always know someone. You should try

Cave of Wonders. The owners are pretty knowledgeable about stones since that's basically all they sell."

"They sell rocks?"

"Yup."

"Where is it?" I asked. "And why haven't I heard of it?"

Kami sighed. "It's not a secret. I've just never had a reason to mention it before now. I had a date take me there once because he wanted to buy me something pretty. There wasn't a second date, but there was a second visit to the shop. And a third and a fourth."

I had a hard time picturing Kami in a shop of pretty rocks. "Do they sell weapons too?"

"Nope. Just a variety of rocks."

"To throw at people?"

Kami shook her head. "Nope."

Cave of Wonders was located at the end of a cobblestone alley. Moisture clung to the air and the alley reeked of mildew. The other shops in the row were vacant except for a nameless one that appeared to specialize in broomsticks. A woman exited the shop as we passed. She had a broomstick tucked her arm and wore a satisfied smile.

"Haggled well?" I asked.

She smiled and displayed only a partial set of teeth. "Too soft for his own good, that one is."

I offered a return smile and kept walking. I hoped she knew a good cloaking spell because the vampire authorities wouldn't be as soft as Calvin. Unless you were a bird or a vampire in butterfly form, flight was prohibited. Even dragons were technically not allowed in Britannia City airspace but good luck keeping them out. All the magic in the world didn't seem capable of that.

Kami and I reached the end of the alley. She nudged open the door, triggering the pleasant jingle of a bell. With a curved ceiling and walls made of gray slate, the shop name seemed appropriate. Two white-haired women greeted us as we entered. Other than the fact that one was a good six inches taller than the other, they looked almost identical.

"Kamikaze, how wonderful to see you. What brings you to the Cave of Wonders today?" the shorter woman asked.

"My friend is looking for information on a stone and I told her you're the experts around here," Kami said.

The taller one squinted at me. "What kind of stone, sweetness? Is it one like you see here?" She waved a hand in the direction of the shelves that were lined with all manner of rocks. Pink ones glittered. Black ones sparkled. The inventory seemed to be organized by category, but I couldn't tell at a glance what those categories were. "If not, perhaps I can interest you in one of our specialty stones instead."

I offered a polite smile. "Trust me. Whatever you have here isn't comparable."

"We'd like information on a stone that drives men crazy," Kami said.

A small smile stretched the shorter one's lips until they practically blended with her skin. "Oh, I see. Tell me, is there a special man in your life? Lovely women like you—surely there must be someone." Her smile widened. "Hopefully many someones."

Her sister scoffed and waved a dismissive hand at me. "Oh, please, Sigrid. Look at this one. No meat on her bones. An axe on her back. There's only a cat that awaits her at home."

My hands flew to my hips. "Hey! There's more than just a cat."

Sigrid lit up. "I knew it!"

"Not a man. A pygmy goat, a red panda, a hen..." I ticked off the other types of animals on my fingers.

The witch's smile shortened. "Now I see why you're in need of a yoni egg."

"A yoni egg?" I hadn't heard of a yoni bird.

The sisters exchanged knowing smiles and Sigrid clapped her hands. "Come, come. Evanka and I will show you."

Kami and I followed them to an aisle at the far end of the shop. Evanka gestured to a row of polished stones. They were oblong in shape and came in a variety of colors and sizes, all smaller than my fist.

"These are made of jade or quartz," Sigrid said.

"They're pretty, but I'm not in the market for trinkets."

"Oh, these are not trinkets, sweetness," Evanka said. "These are for practical use."

Kami scrutinized the smooth stones. "I believe what we have here is a failure to communicate."

"You said you need a stone that drives men crazy." Evanka tapped the shelf. "Trust me. Improve your vaginal performance and watch him go wild."

Kami slapped her forehead. "We're not here for that."

Sigrid blew a raspberry. "Nonsense. Every woman wants to improve vaginal performance."

I stared at the polished stones. "Yoni eggs are…They go…"

Kami nodded and pointed to her nether regions.

"Use them for Kegel exercises," Evanka said. "Very effective."

I grimaced. "That doesn't seem hygienic."

"You clean them after use," Sigrid advised. "They increase your libido."

"Also shortens the menstrual cycle. Helps make you less interesting to vampires," Evanka added.

Kami shot me an apologetic look. "We're not here for a magic vagina stone."

"It's a specific stone," I said. "With markings on it."

Evanka folded her arms and huffed. "What does this specific stone look like? Can you draw it?"

"No. I've never seen it."

Sigrid scrunched her nose. "You're looking for a stone you've never seen? Why?"

"It's a long story." I glanced at the polished stones. "Why do they call them yoni eggs?"

"'Yoni' is an ancient Indian word for 'sacred space,'" Evanka said.

I instinctively squeezed my thighs together. I was so glad Kami was with me today and not Callan. The vampire would've had a field day in the shop. He likely would've slipped a yoni egg into my pocket when I wasn't paying attention. The idea of the prince's hand in my pocket made my cheeks warm and I quickly brushed the thought aside.

"Have you ever heard of a substance that causes werewolves to lose control over their ability to shift?" I asked.

Evanka smirked. "That's called alcohol. Impacts their performance in other ways, too."

Kami seemed to sense we were barking up the wrong tree. "Thanks for your help, ladies. I think we have what we need."

"Are you sure we can't interest you in anything today?" Sigrid asked. She motioned to my hands. "Looks like someone could use a pumice stone for those calluses."

I splayed my fingers and examined the dry, cracked skin.

"Removes dead skin," Evanka added.

Sigrid held up a handful. "With your skin, you'll need more than one. You should probably use it every day, but stop if it makes you bleed. You don't want an infection."

"Or to attract vampires," Evanka said in a low voice.

Kami clamped a hand on my shoulder. "Oh, my friend doesn't need any help in that department."

I shook off her hand and smiled at the witches. "I'll take the lot."

13

Hole took the term 'dive bar' to another level. Broken floorboards. Spiderwebs. Rowdy customers. A jukebox that only played classic rock from pre-Eternal Night.

The bar was owned by a portly werewolf named George. If you considered running out on your bill, he could shoot you from behind the counter before you made it the door. His cache of weapons was hidden in plain sight, tidied away behind a red and white gingham curtain on George's side of the counter.

He knew my name but knew better than to use it. He also knew I came here to be anonymous, like many of his patrons. Usually I came here to meet clients sent to me by Mack Quaid, a Knight of the First Order. But not today.

Today I'd invited Mack himself.

"Thanks for meeting me."

The knight surveyed the shabby interior. "Hole is... pretty descriptive."

"Which is why I don't need to worry about vampires

here." They tended to avoid dive bars, especially in this part of the city. "I need information."

"Why not meet me at my office?" He sniffed the glass of ale we'd gotten from the bar. "The drinks are less stale there."

"In the off-chance I'm being watched, I thought it best to meet somewhere discreet." There was no reason to think Maeron had stopped sending his spies after me. If there was another powerful stone in the mix, I didn't want the prince to know about it.

Mack unfolded his napkin and tucked it into his shirt like he was ready to take down a plate of spaghetti in an Italian restaurant. He was the kind of man who was popular in any setting. Broad shoulders and a mischievous smile made him popular socially. Skill with a blade made him popular among knights. A round, cheerful face, ruddy cheeks, and an open wallet made him popular at the pub.

Mack cocked his head. "Who's watching you?"

"Doesn't matter." The answer risked revealing more than I was inclined to share, not that I didn't trust Mack. He and I met three years ago on an assignment in Camden when we'd been given the same job by the same client. I won that competition and impressed Mack in the process. Now if there was a job he couldn't assign to his own banner for one reason or another, he sent it my way.

"Okay, what kind of information are we talking about then?"

"I need an expert on ancient stones. A real expert," I added hastily, remembering Kami's idea of one.

He gulped down the ale and grimaced. "Stars above, I think this guy needs a new supplier."

"George tries to keep this bar vampire-free, which means certain professional sacrifices."

"Clearly." He wiped his mouth with the napkin. "Yeah, I know someone."

"Thought you might."

"Her name is Antonia Birch."

I raised my eyebrows. "Former girlfriend?"

"Occasional client."

"Phew. Good. I don't have time for an inquisition."

Mack groaned. "It was one time and Geneva was a little bit obsessive."

"A little bit obsessive is like saying she was a little bit pregnant."

Mack wrapped his hands around the glass and exhaled. "She never got over the breakup."

"No kidding. She still carried a photo of the two of you in her wallet." I nursed my glass of ale. I wasn't in the mood to drink. "Tell me about Antonia."

"You can find her at the Britannia Museum. She's a curator there."

"What kind of work have you done for her?"

He fiddled with his napkin. "Technically it's for the museum, but she's my contact. The museum likes to keep any theft of artifacts quiet, so they don't go through official channels. If they report it to the authorities, it'll end up a PR nightmare."

"I'm touched that you trust me enough to share her name."

Mack's friendly expression faded. "If I didn't trust you, I wouldn't work with you."

"Same."

He offered a crisp nod. "And this is why we get along so well." He pulled a card from his pocket and passed it to me. "Give her this so she knows you're legit."

I glanced at the business card with its logo of crossed flaming swords. "Look at you. Such a professional."

"Hope she can help with your secret project."

I could tell Mack was dying to know the details, but it was best to leave him in the dark. If my theory proved correct, I didn't want word of their existence to leak to the masses. In the wrong hands...

It didn't bear thinking about.

I left Mack to finish his ale alone and headed to the museum. The building was located in Russell Square, not far from my flat near Euston Station. Although it incurred damage during the Great Eruption, House Lewis saw fit to restore the museum to its former glory and it continued to showcase antiquities from around the world. Throughout my childhood, my mother and I admired its many collections. It wasn't unusual for her to stand in front of the same display for an hour imparting every related fact she knew. I served as the repository of her knowledge. As a teacher, she said she felt a sense of duty to pass on all that she'd learned, but sometimes I sensed there was more to it than that. On occasion my mother would stand in front of an artifact and trip over her words in a hasty effort to release them, as though there was a ticking clock that no one could hear except her.

I approached the grand columns with the same sense of wonder I had as a child. My mother told me the style was called Greek Revival and meant to emulate classic Greek architecture. Many ancient Greek structures were destroyed beyond repair during the Great Eruption and it was strange to think that the only evidence of their existence might be in photographs and buildings like this one.

I took my time walking through the museum on my way to find Antonia. It was impossible for me to enter a museum and not pause to explore the collections. House Lewis paid for temporary exhibits that arrived from across the globe and those were always worth a gander. Most of the time it was the only way you'd ever lay eyes on a mask from an ancient African vampire tribe, for instance. The colorful masks were designed with strategic holes that aligned with the wearer's fangs. I still remembered staring in awe at the collection and my mother reeling off more facts than my tiny head could carry at the time.

Rhea Hayes was a complicated woman. She would speak about vampires until your ears bled, but only in a general sense. She never revealed anything specific about my father including his name. She shared so many details about vampires that I was certain she'd one day slip and say more about him than she intended, but she never did. As far as she was concerned, the knowledge was too dangerous for me. She worried I'd grow up, bang on his door to announce my existence, and get myself killed in the process.

I stopped in front of a security guard and flashed a friendly smile. Security guards in a place like this were usually one of two types—vampires who could use their speed and strength to protect the museum's contents, or witches and wizards who could use magic. The fact that this guard was short and lean with no discernible fangs suggested he was a wizard.

"Hello, I'm looking for Antonia Birch."

The guard barely made eye contact. "Egypt."

"Thank you."

I didn't need to read a map. I knew exactly where to find the Egyptian and Sudanese antiquities.

In the gallery I spotted a woman on her knees in front of a display. Her black skirt was long enough to cover her butt as she wiggled and twisted. Her lanyard hung backward around her neck, which was how I knew I'd found Antonia Birch. According to the display information, she was adjusting a hieroglyphic tablet that showed early evidence of vampires.

"You know it's crooked now, right?" I asked.

She craned her neck to look at me. With reddish brown hair, deep brown eyes, and unlined fair skin, she was younger and more attractive than I expected.

"It's meant to be at an odd angle," Antonia said. "Someone keeps coming along and straightening it and then I change it back."

"Might want to leave a note that says 'Do Not Touch.'"

"I feel like it should be implicit in that it's a museum artifact."

I offered my hand and helped her to her feet. "Are you Antonia Birch?"

She dusted off her pale pink blouse. "I am. How can I help you?"

I produced the card from Mack. "We have a friend in common. He seems to think you can help me."

Her expression didn't change. She simply handed the card back to me and watched me expectantly.

"I'm looking for a stone," I said.

"Then you've come to the right place." She motioned to the next room. "I'm guessing it's the Rosetta Stone. It's our most popular one."

As fascinating as it was, I'd seen the Rosetta Stone more times than I could count.

"Would it be possible to speak in private?"

Her eyes sparkled with interest. The request clearly intrigued her. "Absolutely. Come with me."

Her heels clicked loudly across the hard floor and I followed her to a door marked 'Staff Only.' She slipped inside and beckoned me forward with a slender finger. Upon closer inspection, I realized the finger was slightly crooked as though a break had failed to heal properly. One of the perils of handling ancient supernatural artifacts no doubt.

The room was the size of a janitorial closet and the shelves were crammed with artifacts the way my pantry was crammed with food containers for the menagerie. There was only one chair which Antonia now sat on. I perched on the pile of empty crates in the corner.

"The stone isn't on display," I explained. "It's a recent discovery. I thought you might know its history."

"Egyptian?"

"I don't know. It was discovered in Devon."

Her brow creased. "And what's so special about this stone?"

I had no choice but to share more. Without enough details, she couldn't help me. "It seems to have a negative impact on werewolves."

Her head jerked slightly. "Can you elaborate?"

"I'd rather not." No need to induce mass panic. Right now there'd been isolated incidents and I didn't want anyone sounding alarm bells.

Her gaze flitted over me. "You're a knight like Mack?"

"Different banner but yes. I need to find this stone. If someone's trying to unload it on the black market, is it the kind of thing you'd know about?"

She shuffled papers around on her desk. "Museum policy prohibits the acquisition of stolen pieces."

"I'm not suggesting you'd buy anything off the black market. I'm only asking if you'd be made aware of its existence. Maybe a contact who tries to sell you items of uncertain origin?"

She clasped her hands on the desk. "Can you at least describe it?"

I described the elemental stone instead. If my theory was correct and the missing stone was related to the other two, then they'd share certain characteristics.

Antonia's eyes seemed to grow wider with each additional detail.

"I love my job," she said, once I'd finished.

Hope flared. "You know something?"

"I know lots of somethings. Are you familiar with the story of the Tower of Babel?"

"Of course."

"Don't say of course," she admonished me. "It's a fair question in this day and age and you're what?" She scrutinized me. "Twenty-six?"

"Thirty."

"Hmm. You're closer to my age than I thought." She slipped on a pair of glasses and selected a book from the pile on the corner of the desk.

"You keep a Bible on your desk?"

She glanced up at me. "As you can see, I keep a lot of books on my desk. Tell me what you know about the tower."

That was easy. My mother's interest in history encompassed world religions as well. She often said it was impossible to separate one from the other.

"The Babylonians got too big for their britches and wanted to build a tower that reached the heavens. God wasn't thrilled with their plan and disrupted the work."

She smiled. "The best laid plans. Go on."

"God confused the language of the workers so they couldn't understand each other and the tower was never completed."

Her eyes blazed with equal parts intelligence and excitement. "Have you ever heard of the Great Pyramid of Cholula?"

I tried to pull the name from my memory bank but came up blank. If my mother knew of it, she hadn't seen fit to impart that particular nugget of wisdom.

"No. It's similar to Babel?"

"A certain North American culture believed that, at the first sign of light upon the earth, giants went in search of its source."

"They went to find the sun?"

She nodded. "They realized it wasn't within reach and so they built a pyramid to use as a ladder."

I thought of the Tower of Babel. "Let me guess. It didn't end well."

"No, certainly not. The giants upset a god of the heavens and the pyramid was destroyed and its inhabitants scattered."

"Sounds about right. Gods are a testy bunch."

She smiled. "There are other versions of the story in cultures around the world. Did you know that?"

"No, but I don't see what that has to do with the stone. The shifters aren't suddenly speaking French. They're..." I stopped short. "It's a behavioral issue."

"It doesn't take a genius to figure out they're losing control. Are they killing others?"

I released a breath. If Antonia had knowledge that might shed light on the bigger picture, then I had to offer more information.

"It isn't just that they're losing control and attacking others. They're losing control of their bodies. They can't choose when to shift in either direction. They go..."

"Berserk," she finished for me. "I've heard of berserkers. I didn't realize there was a connection, but it makes sense."

"Makes sense how?"

"There's a reference to another story somewhere in here." She flicked through the book. "It's called Friseal's Temple."

"Never heard of it."

"If your stone is what I think it is, that means there are others."

"Others? Like maybe a stone with elemental magic?"

She lit up. "Yes. Elemental. And I think the one you've discovered is transcendence. There are three other types if I recall correctly." Her fingers trembled with excitement as she flipped to the index. "Hang on. Let me find the right section. What an incredible discovery."

One of the three remaining types had to be the immortality stone. That meant there were two more powerful stones, yet to be found. If this story was accurate, it could change the world as we knew it.

Antonia turned back to the middle of the book. "Here it is."

The sound of alarm bells jolted us.

Surprise etched Antonia's features. "Must be genuine. There's no drill on the schedule."

Keeping ahold of the book, she began to gather items on her desk in a hurried fashion. "There's a staircase further along the corridor that will get us out faster."

I held out my arms. "Tell me what to carry and I'll help."

She handed me a stack of folders from the desk. "This way." She rushed past me and I quickly followed.

We entered the corridor and I was surprised to see it empty. Shouldn't everyone be evacuating? I sniffed the air. No smell of smoke.

I glanced at Antonia. "It was the fire alarm, wasn't it?"

"I assume so. Security would handle any other kind of threat."

Unless this was security's way of warning us that they'd failed.

We turned the corner and ran into a guard. "What's going on? Where's Reginald?"

The stout man shrugged. "Not sure. Seems to be an unscheduled drill. They sent me up here to remind everyone to lock their office door."

Antonia blinked. "Oh, dear."

"No worries." The guard angled his head toward the exit. "You should keep going, miss. I'll escort Ms. Birch back to her office and make sure she gets safely out of the building."

"I'll stay with you," I said.

Antonia shook her head. "Absolutely not. I'm not aware of any drill and I won't be responsible for risking your safety."

I clutched the folders to my chest. "I'll keep these until I find you."

Once outside, it was clear the security team had no idea what was happening. This wasn't a planned drill, nor was there evidence of a fire. I frowned when I noticed a security guard being treated for a wound on the back of his head.

"Are you sure you didn't fall, Reginald?" another guard asked.

Scowling, Reginald rubbed his head. "I know when I've been whacked on the back of the head, Clive."

Where's Reginald?

Oh, no.

I thrust the stack of folders at the nearest person and sprinted back into the building, ignoring the demands to stop. I raced along the corridor and back to Antonia's office. The curator's shoes were visible from behind the desk.

No, no, no.

I rushed around the desk. Blood streaked down her neck and through her hair.

"Antonia?" I crouched beside her, my heart pounding. Her wide eyes stared back at me, unblinking.

"I'm so sorry," I whispered.

If the alarm was a ruse, what did they want? No one knew why I was coming here except Mack and even he didn't know the full story. Besides, there was no way he violated my trust. That meant someone had been following me and likely eavesdropped on our conversation.

Maeron was the obvious choice, but only because he'd sent spies after me before. But why would he order his goon to kill Antonia?

I looked at the items scattered on the floor beside her and then at the contents on the desk. No doubt about it.

The book was gone.

14

Unsurprisingly, the guard I met in the corridor was nowhere to be found. He'd likely knocked out Reginald and then killed Antonia. I turned invisible and fled the scene before the authorities arrived. If they identified me later and wanted to interview me—I'd cross that bridge if and when I came to it. Right now I couldn't afford to be waylaid. I sent a text to Mack to tell him the sad news. I hoped he didn't blame me.

Why kill Antonia and steal the book? To silence her? Did the killer have the transcendence stone or know its location? If only I'd had more time to read the book before the alarm sounded. At least I had a new lead, although the price had been steep and Antonia had been the one to pay it.

I thought of the elemental stone hidden in my flat and my shoulders grew tense. The situation was so much bigger and more dangerous than I realized. I wasn't sure it made sense to keep the stone in my flat anymore. My ward was tough, but somebody could simply destroy the building if they wanted access badly enough. On the other hand, where else would the stone be safe?

Nowhere.

I'd have to keep it for now until I came up with a better plan.

I walked at a hurried pace in an effort to put distance between myself and the museum. I couldn't return to pack headquarters with my discovery. It was safer to keep the knowledge to myself for now.

If the killer trailed me to the museum and listened to the conversation, then he knew I was aware of the book and the information it contained. If it was one of Maeron's henchmen, why kill Antonia but not me? Wasn't the knowledge I possessed just as dangerous?

Wasn't *I* just as dangerous?

I mulled over the effects of a transcendence stone. Its influence was likely the reason I was able to transform into multiple versions of myself in The Crown. But why? What kind of magic was that? Yes, it was transformational, but still. There had to be more to it.

As I continued walking, the back of my neck grew cold and an involuntary shiver rattled my body. Slowly I twisted to look behind me and that's when I spotted them.

Two butterflies streaked through the air behind me.

My palms started to sweat and I jerked my head forward, pretending not to notice them. Between my weapons and my magic, I could take two without help, although I'd like to know why they were following me. More assassins?

I picked up the pace and rounded the corner. I wouldn't be able to lose them, but if I could get to a busier location, they might be less tempted to take their vampire forms.

I spared a glance over my shoulder and two butterflies had become four.

Terrific.

Four butterflies meant they were vampires trying not to draw attention to themselves. They obviously didn't know about my detection skill.

I hurried through a busy intersection, knocking shoulders and jostling elbows. The crowd slowed me down and the butterflies managed to get ahead of me.

If they wanted to kill me, wouldn't it have made more sense to do it in Antonia's office?

I was relieved to have noticed them before they followed me all the way home. Of course I had the ward in place, but I worried about the menagerie.

I sensed a familiar presence and instinctively looked up to see Barnaby circling above. Good. I needed an airborne ally.

I continued to move through the crowd, my mind calculating my options and their associated risks. A fight in an area like this risked casualties. I couldn't give the butterflies a chance to take shape. On the roof of the building, I spotted a row of pigeons like clothing on a line. I focused on them, sending a mental signal for assistance. Pigeons were easy to convert. Their brains were malleable and they had no ingrained loyalty to a specific species. A small push and I was able to claim them as mine.

One by one the pigeons dove from the edge of the roof. Before the butterflies realized what was happening, they were entangled in an aerial battle with a plague of pigeons.

I sprinted ahead to get past them and lose them in the crowd. Even one butterfly on my tail was one too many. One could always signal for reinforcements and the gods knew there was no shortage of vampires in the city.

A tunnel entrance appeared on my right. Not ideal but it would have to do. The butterflies wouldn't expect me to flee danger by courting more danger. Little did they realize I'd take the monsters below over the monsters above any day of the week. Underground monsters didn't care that I was a dhampir. They only cared if they could eat me.

I hustled down the steps two at a time and then used the railing as a slide until I reached the floor. I crouched at the base of the broken escalator and waited. If they came after me, there was a good chance they'd fly straight over my head and keep going. Vampires didn't retain their sharp senses in butterfly form. Small mercies.

I maintained my hunched position for a few minutes and ran through a series of possible defensive moves should the vampires make an appearance. I was so distracted by my mental preparation that I failed to sense the creature encroaching on my hiding spot until it was too late.

I twisted to see two golden eyes with flecks of green glowing in the darkness. From my crouched position, they were slightly above head level. The creature stepped forward to reveal short, ragged black fur and paws larger than my hand with sharp claws extending from their tips. He reminded me of Trio albeit with one head.

"Hey, buddy."

It was hard to tear my gaze away from those captivating eyes. I'd never seen anything like them.

I tried to reach out with my mind to connect with the creature's, but I kept getting distracted by the golden eyes.

As the hellhound crept closer, the eyes grew larger. I remained in a crouched position, transfixed. Every time I attempted to feel for the creature's mind, I got lost in his two pools of golden liquid. If I wasn't careful, I thought I might drown in them.

My mother's voice whispered in my head. A single word long forgotten.

A golden river rushed toward me, swirling around to engulf me.

I reached out...Why was I reaching out? I only wanted to bathe in the shining sea. Nothing more.

So comfortable.

My mother whispered again. *Plat-eye*.

Plat-eye.

I tore my gaze away from the eyes and the golden river retreated. Snapping out of my trance, I snatched my axe from its sheath and sliced through the air sideways. The creature's head landed on the tunnel floor with a soft thud followed by the body. A high-pitched shriek penetrated my eardrums and I watched as a globular spirit squeezed out of the open neck and dissipated into thin air.

I leaned against the wall to catch my breath. Even dead, my mother managed to save my life. I must've been five years old the first time she'd told me about an evil spirit called a plat-eye. It favored a dog shape but only to lure its victims closer until they were completely entranced.

A narrow escape.

As I wiped off the blade of my axe, I emerged from the tunnel. Plat-eyes didn't tend to travel in groups but one couldn't be too careful.

Across the street I noticed the remains of a churchyard. Queen Britannia had ordered the destruction of all the churches when she seized power and bodies were no longer buried within the city walls. Most churchyards had been picked over long ago and stripped of any resources. This one appeared to be no exception.

Faint movement drew my eye and I saw butterflies flit through the bars of the iron gates as though the rubble was their destination.

Let the hunted become the hunter, I thought with a certain satisfaction. They'd never expect me to follow them. Maybe they'd take me straight to their leader. I'd find out who was responsible for sending them after me and make sure it didn't happen again.

I sprinted across the street and maneuvered between two broken bars. I stopped short when a familiar figure came into view. Pulse racing, I ducked behind a pile of discarded headstones.

Where are you going, Adwin, my vintner friend?

The royal winemaker paused outside the rubble and cast a furtive glance over his shoulder before proceeding. I counted to ten in my head before following him.

The smell of damp oak hung heavy in the air. I watched as Adwin lit a torch on the remnants of the wall and carried it along a narrow corridor. What could he possibly be doing here and where were the other vampires?

Darkness swallowed him and I realized he'd descended a set of hidden steps. I crept behind him, following the light from the torch.

I felt torn. Adwin seemed perfectly nice for a vampire. I longed to waltz up to him and politely request answers. The part of me that saw Antonia Birch's dead body, however, told the polite part of me to shut the hell up.

Slowly I withdrew my dagger.

At the base of the steps I observed him hook the torch on the wall and turn away.

I pounced.

I heard the vampire's sharp intake of breath. "Who's there?"

I held the dagger to his throat. "What is this place?"

His voice trembled. "You do remember I'm a vampire. A blade across the neck won't kill me."

"Maybe not, but it will certainly make it difficult to drink the wine you love so much."

"What is it that you need from me, Miss Hayes?"

"Information."

"Why not ask Prince Callan? You two seem to have developed a certain rapport."

I pressed the blade against his skin. Drops of blood bubbled from the flesh wound. "You're keeping a secret from him. What is it?"

He laughed despite his obvious discomfort. "I can assure you there are *many* secrets between His Royal Highness and myself. We're hardly confidantes."

"You're hiding something here. I want to know what it is."

"You've been watching me?"

"I was going to ask you the same thing."

"Why the devil would I be watching you? I'm the royal winemaker. Nothing more."

"I saw butterflies enter this building. Where'd they go?"

"A routine security sweep. They travel through the churchyard and continue on."

Then they weren't after me? "Security for what?"

"Remove the blade and I'd be delighted to answer your questions."

Delighted seemed a stretch, but I lowered my weapon nonetheless. I could take Adwin with both hands tied behind my back if need be. I opted to ease his discomfort and encourage him to talk. I had more questions now than when I entered the churchyard.

He rubbed his neck and offered an anemic smile. "You'd make an adept assassin. I had no idea you were following me and I have experience watching the shadows."

"I'm not an assassin."

"Thank the devil for that."

Adwin removed the torch from the wall again and used it to light up the rest of the room. Everywhere I looked were crates of bottles and oak barrels. More than I could count, in fact.

"Overflow storage? Is the wine cellar at the palace so small?"

He motioned to the nearest barrel. "I'd offer you a drink, but I don't think this would be to your taste."

"I assume it isn't wine."

"Your assumption is correct, although it isn't what you think." He pointed to a shelf with goblets. "May I?"

I stepped away to give him space. He uncorked a bottle and pulled down a goblet from the shelf. The metallic scent of human blood filled my nostrils. He filled the goblet with an inch of crimson liquid.

"Security sweeps and your visits." I frowned. "You come here to check the stock?"

"Regularly."

"Doesn't blood need to be kept in cooler conditions so it doesn't spoil?" The room was cool but not cold enough to keep blood fresh.

"Not this kind." He raised the goblet to his lips and sipped. "Almost ready, this one. Another few days and it'll be exactly right. Then I'll have the bottles transported to a special room in the palace."

His eyes flickered to me. I got the sense he was waiting for me to ask a question. He wanted to tell me, but he also wanted me to work for the answers.

Okay, I'd play. "The special room is the one Callan and I saw you leaving carrying a crate."

"Prince Callan, yes."

Heat rushed to my cheeks. "Yes, of course." I might be

the one holding a dagger, but Adwin just slayed me with two words.

I glanced at the goblet. "This isn't blood from the tribute centers."

He smiled and I was immediately reminded of his blunt fangs. "No, it isn't."

"Does the royal family know?"

"Only Prince Callan."

"If not from the tribute centers, then where?"

Adwin touched the rim of the goblet. "A secret laboratory funded by the prince. The blood is synthetic."

You could've knocked me over with one of Barnaby's feathers. Callan had mentioned a research lab to me when we were trying to learn more about Damascus steel. I'd bet good money it was the same one.

"You're telling me Prince Callan drinks synthetic blood?"

"Yes, and we hope one day the practice becomes widespread." He parted his lips to show off his squared fangs. "Not all vampires find the consumption of human blood palatable."

Wow. To say I was floored was an understatement.

I scrutinized the barrels. "This is a pretty big secret."

"It is. Can I trust you to keep it?"

"I think you must've already decided that I can. Otherwise you would've used that weapon to try to kill me." I gestured to the crossbow hidden behind a barrel but within arm's reach of the winemaker.

His smile broadened. "Do I have your word as a knight?"

"Yes." I had no reason to out Adwin or Callan. As far as I was concerned, this was a secret worth keeping. "This seems like quite the underground enterprise."

"We've been working on formulas for years, trying to perfect it before we attempt a more widespread introduction. We don't want to give the common vampire any reason to reject it."

"This is what you keep in that secret storage room I saw."

He nodded. "Prince Callan had a ward set up that allows me to come and go through the tunnel without anyone being the wiser."

I studied the residue that clung to the glass of the goblet. "For what's it worth, it looks and smells the same to me."

"Ah, but your senses won't be as finely tuned as a vampire's."

Little did he know. "You said 'we.' Who works with you on this?" There was no way Adwin could oversee this enterprise as well as a serve as the royal winemaker to House Lewis.

"I have a team in place. Their identities are unimportant, but they are all carefully selected and committed to a blood-free diet."

"But Prince Callan is your main backer?"

Adwin inclined his head. "It was he who hatched the scheme in the first place, once he realized I shared his misgivings about human blood."

I took a moment to digest the news. The Horror of the Highlands drank synthetic blood. By choice. To say I was blown away was an understatement.

"Our ultimate goal is to create a substance that combines the nutrients of human blood with the look and taste of an excellent vintage."

"But isn't part of the appeal the look and taste of blood?"

He gave me a knowing look. "So some believe, but science tells us that it's our attraction to what's in the blood that informs our senses. I believe that if the nutrients are present in the wine, the vampire's tastes will shift along with them."

My fingers drifted to the top of the barrel. "You could change the world with this." No more tribute centers. No more looking at humans as a food source.

"Which is why we've kept our endeavor secret for so long. Once we finalize the formula and determine that it's fit for the general vampire population, we'll begin to roll it out."

"How do you intend to do that under the nose of House Lewis?"

He clasped his hands in front of him. "What we hope is that the royal family will share our vision of the future and become a partner in its distribution."

And if they didn't, I had no doubt they'd execute Adwin for treason. The royal family could easily consider the secrecy and subterfuge an attack on their House. I wasn't sure what would happen to Callan. They couldn't execute him, but they could certainly invent ways to make his immortal life miserable before the contract was up and he was returned to his birth family in Scotland.

"You've taken an incredible risk."

A smile tugged the corners of his mouth. "Are you talking about the synthetic blood or sharing our secret with you?"

"The more who know, the more likely the secret gets out before you're ready." I couldn't help but feel concerned for the winemaker's safety. "What's your plan if House Lewis doesn't share your vision? You won't be able to put the genie back in the bottle, no pun intended."

"Prince Callan will handle that particular task. He won't reveal my involvement unless and until they express a positive interest in the matter."

Still, Callan would put himself at considerable risk. "How many vampires are out there who share your view, do you think?"

"More than you would expect."

My gaze swept the room. "Will you tell the prince that I know?"

"I shall leave that to you."

I nodded. I wasn't sure whether it made sense to tell him. I didn't want Callan to view me as a threat. Our relationship was complicated enough.

"If there's anything I can do to help with this," I offered. "I'm more than willing."

Adwin's eyes grew round. "You would risk your life for a cause that doesn't affect you?"

"We're all connected, Adwin. Just because I'm not going to end up at a tribute center doesn't mean I have no stake in the outcome."

The vampire's features softened. "I knew I liked you from the first."

A thought occurred to me. "You served as the royal winemaker under Queen Britannia, too, didn't you?"

His chest inflated. "I did."

"What was your relationship like with her?"

He chortled. "What do you think it was like? She was the queen and I was a lowly member of staff."

"But by all accounts, she loved her wine. You must have been among her favorites."

Adwin's face tightened. "The queen had no favorites."

"What about her relationship with the king? Do you think they loved each other?"

Adwin eyed me closely. "What's this about?"

"My curiosity."

He exhaled. "I suppose you've heard the rumors then."

"Enlighten me."

"There have been whispers over the years that the queen's murder was plotted by her husband and House Duncan. That they used the battle as a cover for their plan."

"Do you believe it?"

"I don't give it much thought. My mind is preoccupied with other matters."

I balked. "You don't think it's important that the king conspired with a rival House to murder his wife?"

Adwin regarded me. "And what if he did? You think King Casek should be made to step down? Who would replace him—Maeron? Do you think the realm would be better off?"

"You think the truth is unimportant?"

"I think the truth's importance is relative to the outcome. Maeron is not ready to be king and the realm is not ready for another war."

He made a good point. If the other Houses saw the potential to launch an attack on Britannia City, they'd seize it with gusto.

"King Casek is a fine vampire," Adwin continued, "regardless of any questionable decisions he may or may not have made. This is a subject I'd leave well enough alone, Miss Hayes."

"You disliked the queen."

"I don't know a living being who felt otherwise. She was a tyrant. Her ego would've doomed us all."

"She rebuilt this city after the Great Eruption," I countered. "She fought for and defended the largest territory in the country." I wasn't sure why I suddenly felt compelled to defend the ruthless vampire queen. Maybe it was the simple fact that, historically, powerful women were torn down far more frequently than their male counterparts.

"And she would've destroyed it eventually, had she been allowed to continue as queen. I'd stake my life on it. I have no interest in dragging what sins that may have been committed into the light. Let them remain ambiguous and in the shadows where they belong." He lifted the torch in a way that displayed our shadows on the stone wall. "That's what I do, Miss Hayes, and I'd advise you to do the same."

15

I retreated to my flat to process the day's events, which involved recounting every detail to the menagerie. Big Red was the only one who bothered to listen all the way through. The others only feigned interest until I gave them their treats, then they wandered away in search of a more stimulating environment. Traitors. The red panda had more patience.

"So those butterflies weren't trailing me," I said, as I stood at the stovetop and cooked a small pot of pasta. "I know what you're thinking—who killed Antonia Birch and why?" I bent over to pat Big Red's head. "No idea yet, but..."

The red panda grunted and skittered out of the kitchen before I could finish.

I walked into the living room where the rest of the animals were quietly gathered in front of the door. Herman bleated.

Okay, someone was outside the door. I waited a few seconds to see whether anyone knocked.

Nope. Silence.

I didn't detect any vampires.

I connected to my magic. After what happened with Antonia at the museum, I had to be careful. If someone killed her and stole the book to suppress the origin story of the stones, then I was in danger.

I leaned forward to peer through the peephole. A man was crouched in front of the door. Although I couldn't see his face, I didn't need to. The sun tattoo on his bald head told me who it was.

The Green Wizard.

I'd encountered him on the site of the former St. Paul's Cathedral where he tried to kill me. Callan had taken out his men and the wizard had teleported to safety.

What was he doing outside my flat?

The door was heavily warded, although he didn't seem to be trying to penetrate it.

He resumed an upright position and a brown eye peered back at me through the peephole.

"I know you're watching me."

"You're sneaking around outside my flat," I replied. "Of course I'm watching you."

"You're London Hayes of the Knights of Boudica, yes?"

I placed a hand on the door handle. "Who wants to know?"

I didn't wait for a response. I yanked the door open with one hand and grabbed the wizard by the collar of his cloak with the other. I slammed the side of his head against the doorframe.

He gathered his wits and used his smooth dome to head-butt me. Herman bleated his displeasure.

"Stay clear," I told the menagerie. I didn't want them feeling inclined to help.

I hunched over and flipped the wizard onto his back on

the floor, slamming the heel of my boot on his chest to pin him in place.

Hera hissed and I glanced at the sofa. "I appreciate your support but don't get involved."

My raised foot dropped to the floor. I glanced down to where the wizard had been lodged beneath my boot only a moment ago.

He reappeared in the kitchen doorway, holding his hands in the air, palms exposed. "Stop. I only want to talk."

Oh, right. The teleporter.

"You weren't so keen to talk last time we met."

"I didn't know."

"Know what?"

I might not be able to teleport, but I was fast. I raced across the room and pushed him against the wall, gripping him by the neck. If I could deprive him of enough oxygen, he wouldn't be able to think straight enough to teleport.

"Why did you kill Antonia Birch? Where's the book?"

"I...don't know...what you mean."

I tightened my grip to the point where his eyes began to bulge. "Why are you here?"

"Look...down. Door."

I cast a glance over my shoulder at the floor to see a small rectangular card. That must've been why he was crouched in front of my door. It couldn't be made of poisoned paper or spelled or it wouldn't have made it through the ward.

Herman started toward the card to investigate.

"Big Red," I called.

The pygmy goat treated any form of paper like a snack. The red panda scooped the card into his mouth and delivered it to my free hand.

I examined the card and then looked at the Green Wizard. "The card is blank."

There was no symbol. No logo. No name.

I released my grip on his neck so he could talk.

"Only practitioners of magic can read what's on the card," he rasped. "It's a failsafe."

"Witches and wizards only, huh?" I turned the card over. "A reveal spell? You've got a giant sun tattoo on your head, but you need to keep your business cards a mystery? Seems to me you're a walking billboard."

I let him go.

"I'm part of a group called PSR," he said, rubbing his neck.

I tried to identify the meaning of the letters. Post-Sun Revolution? No. Please Stop...'Pocalypse?

I gave up. "I've got nothing."

"People in Support of Ra. Our main objective is to bring back the sun."

I barked a laugh. "How do you expect to do that? A really tall ladder?"

"We thought we could use the elemental stone."

"Except you don't control it."

"An unfortunate turn of events thanks to you."

If he was trying to guilt me, it didn't work. "You should've joined forces with the druid. That's why he wanted it, too."

"Dashiell wanted power. Nothing more."

On that we agreed.

I closed the door and sat on the sofa next to Hera. "You said you thought you could use the elemental stone. You don't believe that anymore?"

"We no longer believe the stone is enough on its own."

I stroked the cat's back and she responded by biting my hand. "I'm afraid I can't help you."

"Can't—or won't?"

I arched an eyebrow. "Does it matter?"

"We'd like to extend an invitation to you to join our group."

"I'm not much of a joiner."

"You're a knight."

"Out of necessity. A girl has to eat."

He looked down at the animals that had collected at his feet. It wasn't every day I had guests in the flat. "We could use someone with your skills."

"I hate to undermine what your mother told you, but you're not special. Everyone could use someone with my skills."

His eyes met mine. "But is everyone trying to bring back the sun and eliminate vampire rule? Perhaps I'm biased, but I believe our cause is worthier than any other use of your skills."

He had a point. The return of sunlight to the realm would be...Well, it was impossible to overstate its significance. It would change life as we know it, just as the sun's disappearance changed life for previous generations.

"Okay, I'll bite. How do you propose to bring back the sun?"

"Meet us and find out." He motioned to the card. "The next meeting is tomorrow. That's why I came here now. To invite you to attend."

"I'll think about it."

He frowned. "You fight alongside vampires and yet you refuse a simple meeting with your own kind?"

"Trust me. You're not my kind."

"I've seen evidence of your magic."

"That doesn't mean we're the same."

Although I put on a good show, his words hit too close for comfort. Why was I willing to extend a certain amount of trust to Callan and House Lewis, yet unwilling to do the same for the Green Wizard? He was right. I had at least as much in common with him as I did with vampires.

He started toward the door. "If you're not with us, then you're against us. It's that simple."

"The world is literally awash in shades of gray. Nothing is that simple." I tossed the card on the coffee table. "What's your name?"

"Joseph Yardley."

"I think I'll still call you the Green Wizard. It's catchier."

He offered a half smile. "I don't really mind what you call me as long as you join the cause."

I SLEPT like a corpse that night and when I awoke the next day, I made the decision to attend the meeting. I couldn't share the information I'd learned about the stones with the Green Wizard, but maybe there was something I could learn from them. I was curious to know more about their plan. Just because they wanted to overthrow vampire rule didn't automatically make them a better option. I needed to know more.

A basic reveal spell gave me the time and location of the PSR meeting. If I were Joseph Yardley, I would've chosen a more memorable abbreviation for my group, but hey, I wasn't in charge of the marketing department.

I debated inviting Kami to go with me, but, in the end, I went alone. Yardley had only extended the invitation to me and I wasn't sure how an extra guest would go over. He trusted me enough to include me, but that didn't mean I trusted him. The only thing I trusted were the weapons strapped to my back. And to my thigh.

And my ankle.

Finally I was ready.

I triple-checked to make sure I wasn't being followed today. I didn't want to be the reason the Green Wizard's party was busted by vampires.

The meeting was being held in the Barbican. Not too far and there was a direct bus from Euston.

On the bus I took a seat beside an elderly woman with a shopping bag. She cut a quick glance at my axe and shuffled closer to the window.

I smiled. "Blind date. A girl can't be too careful these days."

She averted her gaze and stared out the window instead.

My phone buzzed with an incoming message from Kami. I'd deal with her later.

I disembarked at the Barbican stop and noticed the same elderly woman struggling with her shopping.

"Need any help? I can carry that for you if you like."

Her eyes turned to slits. "Do I look like I was born yesterday?"

More like one hundred yesterdays, but I thought it best not to comment.

"If I wanted to steal it, I would've done it already, but if you don't want help, that's fine. I get it." I held up my hands and turned to walk away.

"It's only two blocks," she called after me. "Think you can manage?"

I swiveled around and she thrust the bag toward me. I looped the handle over my shoulder. "Holy hellfire. What have you got in here? Rocks?"

"A set of hand weights."

I smiled. "You're going to start working out?" Better late than never, I guess.

"I intend to use them as weapons on intruders. A wolf went crazy in the lobby of my building. It took several residents to tackle him."

A berserker in this area now? The stone's influence or a coincidence?

"Who was he?"

"Heck if I know. We only have one wolf in the building. Lives in the penthouse suite and we rarely see him. All I know is it wasn't him."

"What happened to the crazy wolf?"

"Don't know. After he was knocked unconscious, somebody called pack authorities to report the incident."

I'd have to check in with Romeo and see whether another wolf was brought to the infirmary. He wasn't there when I spoke with Rafe. Maybe he was brought in later.

The elderly woman stopped in front of a building. The sign over the entrance canopy read Acadia.

"Here we are. I'll make it the rest of the way."

I handed her the bag. "Good luck. I hope you never have to use those weights."

She smiled. "I hope you never have to use that axe."

If only.

I continued another block and down a side street to the address on the card. I didn't need to check the numbers to know where I was going.

Halfway down the street I spotted two hulking men. It wasn't my business, but if they wanted to keep this meeting secret, posting two burly guards in plain view wasn't the right way to go about it. If a vampire patrol caught sight of them, they'd be curious to know exactly what Humpty and Dumpty were guarding.

"How's everyone this fine day?" I asked. "I just helped an old lady carry her bag. I figure there must be a kitten in a tree just around the corner."

"Card," the man on the left growled.

I showed them the card Yardley had given me. Grunting, they moved aside to let me pass.

The room's low ceiling prompted me to duck even though there was plenty of space for me to stand at full height. Wooden beams ran the length of the ceiling and I tried to figure out what the room's purpose might've been once upon a time. Before I could reach a conclusion, a bell clanged and Joseph Yardley a.k.a. the Green Wizard took his place at the head of the room like a teacher ready to launch into a lecture. He wore his trademark green cloak and the sun tattoo on his head gleamed in the dim light.

There were about twenty-five people seated, ranging in age from an acne-riddled teenager to a white-haired woman with deep creases in her face and a hunched back. A cane rested against the edge of her chair.

"Welcome, friends," he began.

I listened to his impassioned speech and watched the faces of his listeners as they flickered from interested to angry to hopeful. Yardley seemed to know how to hit all the right emotional buttons. On the surface he didn't say anything I disagreed with, but I already knew who, what, and why. I was more interested in how and when.

I didn't hear those answers.

Afterward, I lingered in the back row and waited for the crowd to depart. Yardley remained deep in conversation with a handful of other attendees wearing similar cloaks. Of the twenty-five attendees, I only counted three women.

"You need more witches," I commented.

Yardley's brown eyes twinkled. "Which is why I invited you, remember?"

The lone woman in the huddle stuck out her hand. "I'm Susan Mayflower."

"London Hayes." Her skin was dry and cool and slightly calloused.

"You're thinking about this all wrong," a man in a brown cloak continued. "Why wouldn't I be able to have elemental powers if I possessed the elemental stone?"

"Because the evidence suggests that's not how it works, Byron," Susan said, clearly irritated by her friend's refusal to accept the information. "If you don't have elemental magic in your bloodline, the stone does nothing for you."

"The stone does nothing for any of us because we don't have it," someone else complained.

"That stone could be our ticket to the top of the food chain." Byron jabbed a finger in the air to emphasize the point.

I looked more closely at him. His thick brown hair covered his head like a helmet and his nose was wide and flat like he'd pressed his face against a window too long and it stayed that way.

"Not anymore," Susan said. "House Lewis will make sure that stone never sees the light of day." She laughed at her unintentional joke.

"What do you know about the stone?" I asked.

Their gazes turned to me. "It brought back Damascus steel," Byron said.

"I know it expanded a magic user's elemental powers, but what about the bigger picture? Where did it come from? Are there more?" I didn't want to specifically ask about Friseal's Tower. I needed to research on my own first.

Byron itched his nose. "If there's more than one elemental stone, I hope it turns up soon."

Brown Cloak balled his hands into fists. "If only we'd gotten our hands on that one at St. Paul's. Would've changed everything."

An image of Callan making short work of Yardley's companions flashed in my mind and I lowered my head.

"I should go. It was nice meeting you." I turned toward the exit and Yardley fell in step with me.

"I see the sorrow in your eyes. What happened at St. Paul's was unfortunate but understandable. You were hunting a murderer. You didn't realize our interests were aligned."

I pivoted to face him. "I'm still not certain they are."

Yardley flinched. "Surely now that you've listened...You must realize it makes sense to join us."

I folded my arms. "And what happens if I don't? Will you really decide I'm against you?"

His expression darkened. "Let's hope we never have to find out."

16

I left the meeting feeling slightly uneasy thanks to the Green Wizard's parting words. As I started in the direction of the bus stop, my phone buzzed with another incoming message from Kami.

"Hey. Sorry, I meant to call you earlier. What's up?"

"Where are you?"

"The Barbican. Why?"

"Damn. I thought you might be home."

"She's still closest!" Briar's voice rang out.

"Closest to what?"

"Can you head over to Hampstead Heath?" Kami asked.

I groaned. "Gerald Latham again?"

"He said he's trapped the monster behind his house and wants us to come dispose of it."

I could practically hear the air quotes around 'dispose.'

"Trapped it how?"

"I don't know, but take a picture when you find out. I want to experience it like I was there."

"Why can't you?"

"Briar and I are dealing with a family of centaurs who

enjoyed too many mimosas at brunch. The owner of the restaurant offered to pay double our fee if we get them out before the lunch crowd wanders in."

"Have fun with that." Drunken centaurs were tough to corral. I discovered that the hard way when a bachelor party spilled into Hole one night.

Two short bus rides later and I was at Hampstead Heath standing in Gerald Latham's backyard.

"Up there in the tree," the old man said, pointing to a branch.

I turned on my phone's flashlight app for a better view. Sure enough, an unusually large fox stared back at me.

"You've got to be kidding me." It wasn't a kitten but close enough.

"Can you shoot it from here?" Gerald asked.

"Not even if I had a gun on me. It's just a fox."

His eyes rounded in disbelief. "Just a fox? Have you ever seen a fox that size? Besides, I think it has rabies. I saw it shaking and foaming at the mouth. That means you have a civic duty to get rid of it."

"I don't think a fox that's shaking and foaming at the mouth would have the wherewithal to scramble up a tree and hide," I pointed out.

"I'm telling you, it did. It only stopped shaking when I threw a rock at it. Then it ran up the tree. I don't know why it keeps coming back. We secured the bins." His arms flailed. "Oversized rats and foxes. Missing kids. Vampires moving in. If I could afford to move, I'd be gone already. This city is nothing but a rat-infested cesspool."

An oversized fox behaving erratically.

A missing kid.

New vampire neighbors.

Gods above.

I sucked in a breath. "Mr. Latham, do you happen to recall exactly when the girl went missing?"

"I don't remember offhand. It was the day my new teapot was delivered. Maybe two or three weeks ago?"

The gears in my mind continued to click. "And the vampires next door...By any chance, did they move here from Devon?"

He tugged his earlobe. "You'll have to ask them yourself. It's not like I've invited them 'round for tea and biscuits."

I glanced at the neighboring house. If I was wrong, the worst that could happen was the vampires complained to Mitchell Dansker. He was a powerful vampire, but I doubt he'd care about a random knight casting aspersions on his tenants.

I turned away from the tree and felt Gerald's fingers clutch my sleeve. "Hey, where do you think you're going?"

"To solve your problem." And quite possibly mine.

He jabbed a finger skyward. "My problem's right here in this tree."

"Leave the fox alone, Mr. Latham, and let me do my job."

I stalked across the yard and knocked on the door. The house was similar in appearance to Gerald's red brick Edwardian house. They were likely built around the same time.

The door opened and I smiled at the stout woman who answered.

"Hello. My name is London Hayes and I'm from the Knights of Boudica."

Despite her frown, her expression remained friendly. "Oh, are you soliciting? I thought that was prohibited here."

"I'm not soliciting. I'm investigating a case and...Did your family move here from Devon, by any chance?"

Her friendly demeanor evaporated. "I knew it. What has Trevor done this time?"

"Trevor?"

"My son. Sixteen. Brown hair. Attitude bigger than the Atlantic Ocean." She licked her lips. "You're not here about Trevor?"

"I'm not sure. I might be. May I come in?"

Two minutes later Trevor's mother—Anna—and I were in the living room. I declined her offer of a drink so she popped open a bottle of O-negative for herself and slumped in the chair across from me with a weary sigh.

"Trevor's always been a troublemaker, from the time he was old enough to walk." Smiling, she shook her head. "His father can be a handful and my mother-in-law said he was a dreadful little boy."

"And that's why you left Devon?"

"Trevor was getting a reputation and it started to suffocate us. We decided it was best to start fresh somewhere new. It's not easy to move between territories, as I'm sure you know, but Mitchell Dansker is my husband's cousin and he was able to secure our paperwork and find us this place to live."

"And when did you get here?"

"About three weeks ago." She grunted. "Trevor immediately got in trouble at school for bad behavior. He was changing into a butterfly during class and the teachers were having none of it. I tried to explain that it was the stress of the move, but they refused to listen."

"He was changing form?"

She nodded and took another sip of blood. "I assumed there'd be some repercussions from the move, but I didn't expect it to be spontaneous shape-changing."

"What made you think it was stress? Has he done it before?"

"No, never. I mean, he's always been able to transform, which his father and I were surprised by because neither of us can do it and—I don't know how much you know about vampires—but that ability is genetic."

"Did you take him to see a healer?"

"I did, as a matter of fact, and the healer's the one who identified stress as the cause. Trevor swore up and down he wasn't doing it on purpose."

"What time do you expect him home?"

She cocked her head. "You want to speak to my son?"

I nodded. "I have a few questions that I think only he can answer."

She eyed me suspiciously. "You said he wasn't in any trouble."

"He isn't, but he might be able to help my investigation."

She sipped her blood. "That'd be a nice change. Trevor helping someone other than himself. Might be a good experience for him."

The sound of the front door prompted a smile from her. "Perfect. Here he is now."

Trevor didn't appear to be the troublemaker his mother claimed. In fact, with his boy-next-door good looks, he reminded me of a catalogue model.

"Trevor, this is London Hayes from the Knights of Boudica."

Trevor's gaze traveled over me. "Why are you a knight? Nobody wanted to marry you?"

"You have a very binary perception of women."

His mother clutched her bottle of blood to her chest. "Why don't I leave the two of you alone to talk?" She hurried out of the room.

"I'd like to ask you a few questions about your move from Devon."

His brown eyes glittered with curiosity and intelligence. A combination like that was definitely dangerous in the wrong teenager.

"What's in it for me?"

Naturally. "The opportunity to help the greater good."

He laughed. "No, seriously."

I put my hands on my hips. "Answer the questions because I ask them, Trevor. I don't want to have to resort to threats of violence."

He wore a half smile. "You sort of just did. Clever."

I stayed the course, despite wanting to throttle him. I was beginning to grasp his mother's description. "Tell me about your transformation trouble."

His jaw clenched. "My mother told you about that? That's personal."

I ignored him. "When did it stop?"

He squinted at me. "What makes you think it did?"

"I'm going to guess it started right before you left Devon and stopped about a week ago."

Silence stretched between us. Finally he said, "Sounds about right. Is there something you can tell me about that?"

"You left Devon with a souvenir. Where is it now?"

"I left with an entire collection of souvenirs."

"This one's a stone the size of your foot. Has markings on it."

He balked. "How do you know about that?"

I crossed my arms and stared at him. "Just answer."

He flopped on the sofa in a huff. "I kept it in my schoolbag, but the day I got sent home for improper transformation, I stopped at a pub on my way home for a pint. I only turned my back for a second and somebody nicked my bag."

"Any idea who?"

He shook his head. "I didn't see."

"Was the pub called The Crown?"

He gave me a wide-eyed look. "Yeah, it was. Did you find my bag?"

"No. Where did you find the stone?"

"Some fancy house where humans have no business living. The wall had caved in after a storm and my friends and I went to check it out. I saw the stone and took it."

"There were lots of stones. Why that one?"

He shrugged. "Like you said, it had cool carvings on it. Two snakes twisted together. My parents had already told me we were moving—that's why I was out with my friends commiserating. I took it as a memento."

"And that's when you started having trouble transforming into a butterfly."

"Yeah, it's a cool ability to have. Not all vampires can do it, you know? And suddenly I was getting stuck or changing when I didn't want to." He studied me. "Did the stone do that to me?"

"I think so. That's why I need to find it. It's been hurting others with shifting abilities. There's a fox in the neighborhood that's been getting into the garbage."

"So what?"

"It's not just a fox. It's your missing neighbor, a fox shifter named Kari."

"Why didn't she transform back when I lost the stone?"

Why didn't all vampires within range of the stone turn into butterflies like Trevor did? Lots of questions. Very few answers.

"I don't know. The stone doesn't seem to impact everybody in the exact same way, but Kari's parents have been worried sick and poor Kari is currently hiding up a tree in Mr. Latham's backyard."

He dug a toe into the depths of a thick rug. "What do I care about some shifter?"

"Nothing, I suppose." I rose to my feet. "But I can't knowingly let someone else suffer if I have the ability to help them."

He observed me out of the corner of his eye. "It kind of hurt when I was stuck in my butterfly form. Has she been stuck like a fox this whole time?"

"Ever since you moved in. The neighbor saw her foaming at the mouth. He thought she was rabid and would've killed her."

His gaze dropped to the floor. "Shit." He looked up at me. "What can I do?"

"What else was in the bag? Anything of value?" Anything I could track like a phone?

"Just books for school."

It was just as well. The odds of the stone still being in the schoolbag were slim to none. Whoever had the stone now likely figured out it had power and moved it elsewhere.

"Thank you for answering my questions, Trevor. You've been incredibly helpful."

A smile inched across his face. "Cool."

I returned next-door and bypassed Gerald's buzzer to hit the one for 2A.

A voice crackled through the speaker. "Who's there?"

"Hi, my name is London Hayes with the Knights of Boudica. We met recently by your rubbish bins. I told you about the fox."

The door clicked and I pushed it open, heading straight for the stairs. The woman was waiting for me outside her door. She ushered me inside hurriedly.

"You have news?"

"Yes, but first I need you to come clean. You know where Kari is, don't you?"

She hesitated. "Yes."

"And you know she's the fox we found in your bins."

Tears welled in her eyes as she offered a crisp nod.

"Why not tell your husband? Wouldn't it make him feel better to know his daughter is safe?"

Her voice was low and quiet. "Because then he would know she wasn't his."

Suddenly her earlier behavior made sense. She didn't inquire whether we wounded the fox because she hoped we'd killed it. She wanted to know whether her daughter was injured.

"Why didn't Kari come to you when she got stuck in her fox form? Does she know to hide her identity from her father?"

"No. Kari didn't even know she *was* a shifter." She burst into tears. "This is all my fault. If only I'd been truthful with her. She must be so frightened."

"There are no shifters in the family?"

"My husband and I are human. It's the only world she knows." She broke eye contact again, unwilling to look at me. "The affair was brief but intense. I think him being a fox shifter was part of the allure. I broke it off when my husband started to get suspicious. Once I found out I was pregnant, I ended the relationship. I started giving Kari potions in her bottle to stunt her shifting ability and called them her vitamins. My husband was none the wiser."

"Why not tell Kari?"

"To protect her, of course. If my husband knew the truth…" She sucked in a breath. "I worried he'd take my betrayal out on her. She's almost an adult. I was planning to tell her then. Give her the choice whether to live authentically or not."

"But that choice was taken away."

She nodded. "First by me. Then by whatever spell bypassed the potion and triggered her ability. Once you told me about the fox sighting, I knew it was Kari. I waited until my husband was asleep and then I went to search for her. I've been keeping her safe since then. I think she's afraid to stay in the park. It's too dangerous."

I recommended a wolf wand to see whether it would help her shift back to human form. Now that Kari was away from the stone's influence, it might help her shift back. I suspected it was the girl's inexperience that kept her trapped in fox form. If the wolf wand failed to work, I suggested calling a healer.

Her eyes shone with relief. "Are you sure she can be human again?"

"Yes, I think so."

She buried her face in her hands. "Thank you," she whispered.

I LEFT Hampstead Heath feeling a little lighter than I felt on the way here. I hadn't found the stone, but Trevor's revelation and Kari's imminent return to human form were major steps forward.

As I reached the corner, my phone rang. I pulled it from my pocket expecting to see Kami's name. No Caller ID.

"Hello. I have no interest in extending my car's warranty because I don't own a car," I said.

"Interesting way to answer your phone."

I perked up. "Hey, Romeo. Good timing. I've made real progress today."

"That's terrific. How close are we to that date?"

I snorted. "That's how you measure my progress?"

"If I let you measure me, will that make us even?"

Good grief. "I believe I said let's keep things professional. Speaking of which, why don't I swing by your office and tell you what I found out?"

"I'd love that. Unfortunately I'm not in the office right now."

"I guess that update will have to wait then." I couldn't risk meeting him in a public place where we might be overhead. I wasn't planning to be completely forthcoming, but I certainly didn't want Maeron's spies to eavesdrop on the information I did choose to share.

Romeo hesitated. "If you're willing, you could swing by my place. We'll have privacy, which I assume is what you're after."

"For professional reasons, Romeo," I reminded him.

"Message received." He gave me the address and told me to take the elevator to the 10th floor.

I was basically backtracking to the same area I'd been earlier. Terrific.

"I'll be there as fast as I can."

Two buses and two blocks later and I was back in familiar territory. A little too familiar, actually.

I looked at the number on my phone and looked at the building again.

Arcadia.

I counted the floors. Ten.

Romeo lived in the penthouse.

Huh.

I breezed into the lobby and went straight to the lone elevator. There was no doorman or security guard on duty. I hit the button and traveled to the top.

The doors opened straight into the flat. You would think he'd have tighter security in place given recent events.

"Romeo?" I resisted the urge to call 'where for art thou?'

His penthouse was much nicer than mine. His took up the entire top floor of the building. The walls were almost entirely made of glass, which left little room for artwork or other personal mementos. The furniture was sleek with clean lines and in bold colors like purple and red. I spotted a spiral staircase that appeared to lead to the roof. I felt a pang of jealousy. Although the style didn't appeal to me, his flat could comfortably house my menagerie several times over.

Romeo stepped through a doorway holding two flutes bubbling with pale golden liquid. His trousers were so tight they threatened to rip open and his white shirt was unbuttoned far enough to his expose his broad, hairy chest. Nope. Not my type.

"What part of professional did you misunderstand?"

He grinned and handed me a flute. "Oh, come on. One drink won't kill you."

I held the glass out of politeness, but I had no desire to drink.

Romeo gestured to the purple sofa. "Have a seat and tell me what you've learned. I'm all ears."

I perched on the edge of the cushion and set the flute on the glass coffee table. "Before I start, why didn't you tell me about the wolf in your lobby?"

He appeared momentarily stunned. "I don't know what you mean. What wolf?"

The elderly woman definitely said the pack handled it.

"You had a berserker right here in your lobby."

"How do you know about that?"

I ignored his question. "Why didn't you tell me? I'm supposed to be tracking the pattern of berserkers."

"I figured you had enough on your plate. I was planning to tell you during our next update, which is now." He offered an easygoing smile, but I wasn't buying it. Romeo had no intention of telling me about the berserker in his own building and I was pretty sure I knew why.

"You knew if you told me about him that I'd figure out you're the only wolf living in this building. The last thing you wanted was an investigation on your doorstep." Romeo had been part of the cleanup crew at The Crown. "You found the schoolbag with the stone, didn't you?"

"I was looking for clues to what happened. I unzipped the bag and turned to show Barry, another crew member, but he was already on the floor twitching. He fought the change with every fiber of his being." Romeo dragged a hand through his dark hair. "Man, he couldn't fight it to save his life. I saw the stone and wondered if there was a connection. Wondered why it didn't change me, too."

"So you continued to test it on other wolves and hired me to do your dirty work."

"No, I did the real dirty work, moving the stone around the city to test its effects and the potential radius. I sent *you* to get more information about it."

"But you didn't know about Trevor taking the stone from Albemarle?"

"No, but I knew enough about berserkers to know there was a connection between what was happening in the city and the berserkers in Devon."

"You experimented on your own pack after knowing one had already died?"

"Two now, if you include the one who escaped to the lobby." Romeo shrugged his broad shoulders. "I didn't see a better way. Not all wolves were affected. I wanted to know why." He paused thoughtfully. "Still do."

One who escaped to the lobby? That was the one the elderly lady mentioned.

My head swiveled. Victoria had mentioned missing werewolves. Had Romeo been kidnapping them and bringing them to his flat to test the stone on them?

Bile rose in my throat. "You used me."

"I *hired* you. I wanted to use you, too, but you kept saying no."

Well, at least my romantic instincts were spot on.

An image of Callan surfaced in my mind.

Okay, maybe not.

A question nagged at me. "Why kill Antonia Birch? Is it because she knew too much about the stone?"

His face went blank. "Who's Antonia Birch?"

I didn't know whether to believe him. Until now I wouldn't have pegged Romeo as the kind of werewolf who'd sacrifice members of his own pack, yet here we were.

"The museum curator. You had someone follow me to her office. They killed her and stole a book but left me alive."

Romeo tried to look concerned but finally burst into laughter. "Of course I had to leave you alive. You're doing all that legwork for me." He patted my shoulder. "And very fine legs they are."

"You made it look like a vampire attack."

He made a dismissive sound at the back of his throat. "They deserve it."

"Antonia didn't deserve that."

"Collateral damage, London. She couldn't be trusted to keep her mouth shut. Next thing you know there'd be academic symposiums about powerful stones and everybody and their grandmother would be searching for them. I had to keep this quiet."

"I really wanted you to be one of the good guys." I didn't know how to define that term anymore. Every time I thought I knew, someone like Romeo made me think again. If you'd have told me two months ago about a group trying to bring back the sun and overthrow vampires, I would've said sign me up. But that was before understanding the lengths that people like Dashiell were willing to go to. Before meeting sweet Davina.

And before Callan.

Romeo seemed pained by the statement. "I *am* one of the good guys." His jaw clicked. "I want to take control of the pack and make us stronger. With an army of berserkers, we'd be strong enough to take on House Lewis. With this whole tribunal setup, my hands are tied unless Jervis and Nicolette agree." His scowled. "I can't stand Jervis and Nicolette. They're not leaders. They're glorified bureaucrats."

"Oh, please. This isn't about the pack. You want to use the stone for your own selfish purposes." He was no better than Dashiell.

"I wish things had been different, London. Truly." He strode to the wall and pressed a button. A hidden door slid aside. Howls and screeches emanated from the gaping hole.

A soundproof room?

Romeo ducked into the room and emerged two seconds later with a satchel.

"You want to show off the stone?"

"No. I want to show off what I can do with it."

A werewolf shot out of the room snarling and snapping his jaws. He was stuck between forms, but his face was human enough that I recognized him.

I backed away. "Rafe?" I shook my head. "No. Rafe was better. I saw him."

Romeo patted the satchel. "He was, but I wanted to see

what would happen if I put him closer to the stone again. All in the name of progress."

Rafe's eyes locked on me and he started to salivate.

Romeo sauntered to the elevator. "Good luck, London," he said, pressing the button. "I regret that I didn't get to have sex with you before I let them kill you, but we all have sacrifices to make."

The elevator doors closed as three more berserkers bolted into the living room.

I couldn't take on four berserkers without significant damage. What if the elderly lady lived below Romeo? I didn't want a crazed wolf dropping down from the ceiling. No hand weight on earth would be powerful enough to help her.

I darted past them and scrambled up the spiral staircase to the rooftop. There'd be less chance of injuring any residents up there and the spiral staircase would slow their pursuit of me.

Once outside I spotted Barnaby swooping overhead. The raven must've sensed my distress. No surprise given what I was feeling.

He landed on the rooftop and I waved him away. "Follow Romeo! Big, burly werewolf with a satchel. I need to know where he goes."

The raven spread his wings and flew away.

I sprinted across the rooftop.

Romeo was right. The view from here was incredible. Too bad I couldn't take time to enjoy it.

The wolves fanned out into a semi-circle in the middle of the rooftop, effectively cutting me off from the only exit. For berserkers they were surprisingly coordinated. I had no doubt that with more time, Romeo would've been able to develop the werewolf pack of his dreams.

And my nightmares.

My energy levels began to rise and silver light filtered from my pores. Fear and adrenaline seemed to be triggering a surge of magic.

Creeping toward me, they snapped their jaws in unison.

My body hummed with energy.

Kraken on a cracker. I was going to erupt like a supervolcano. I'd put the whole building in danger if I wasn't careful. I had to maintain control. If I used too much magic, I'd become a force much, much worse than the berserkers. I wanted to stop them without killing them. It wasn't their fault they were trying to hurt me.

Rafe stepped a large paw forward and the others followed suit.

My mind raced through the options. I'd faced off against the berserkers at The Crown and lived to tell the tale. Romeo didn't know about that particular trick up my sleeve. If I could make three more versions of me, then it would be a fair fight.

Rafe lunged.

Too late.

I jumped aside without realizing how close I was to the edge. I wobbled slightly before regaining my balance. Unfortunately, Rafe was also regaining his. Growling, the wolf skidded to a stop and turned to face me. Rafe snarled again and displayed a set of very sharp teeth. Shockwaves of fear pulsed through me and magic flooded my system, seeping into every available pore.

All four berserkers launched themselves at the same time. Five seconds seemed to stretch into five minutes as the world slowed. I watched their giant maws open and their claws slash at the empty air between us. I counted each drop of saliva that sprayed from their eager tongues.

I let the magic go.

Silver light exploded from me. The brightness forced my eyes closed and sharp howls of pain pierced my ears. For a moment, I lost control over my limbs. My arms and legs stretched and stiffened so that I resembled a starfish.

The light faded and I dropped to the floor.

I opened my eyes. Four bodies lay sprawled on the rooftop.

Human bodies.

What did I do?

I crawled over to Rafe. His eyes were closed and I observed his chest rise and fall.

He was alive.

I pulled out my phone and called Kami. "I need everyone on the rooftop of this address. Make sure you bring Briar. They need a healer."

"Who?"

"No time to explain." I gave her the address.

"Will you meet us there?"

"No, I have to go." I hung up the phone and ran to the spiral staircase.

Romeo Rice was going to regret his decision to throw me to the wolves.

Romeo thought I was dead, which meant he wouldn't feel the need to hide. If he did have any lingering doubts about my survival, he'd go to pack headquarters where he'd be protected.

Except he also had the stone. Would he risk bringing the stone into a building full of werewolves? The results would be catastrophic.

I needed to get that stone.

Unfortunately, I'd already sent the knights to deal with the berserkers on the rooftop. A tactical error.

I sprinted down the block with the phone to my ear trying to get ahold of Mack.

No signal.

Because of course there wasn't. Thanks, unreliable satellites.

Barnaby appeared in the sky ahead of me. Looked like my hunch was right.

The raven noticed me and cawed.

Lead the way, friend.

I streaked across the city on foot. With each step my mind replayed what happened on the rooftop. I'd never exploded before. After releasing so much magic, I felt energized. I knew it wasn't normal. My witch friends became drained when they used too much. With me it was like an invitation to a magic rave, which was one of the reasons I fought for control over it. I didn't want to lose myself to magic. I didn't want to hurt anyone.

Well, almost anyone.

Romeo would have no reason to rush. Depending on how he traveled to Sloane Street, there was a chance I could beat him there.

I took every shortcut I could think of. There were benefits to growing up on the streets. You learned to get around the city in a way that most residents were oblivious to.

Barnaby hovered ahead. In the glare of the streetlights, I caught sight of Romeo's tall frame.

Gotcha.

He turned the corner toward pack headquarters. I had to hurry.

I turned invisible and cut through the crowd. I didn't want to risk him glancing over his shoulder to see me.

I rounded the corner and was relieved to see he'd stopped at a food stall. Smart business decision, parking across from pack headquarters. Lots of hungry werewolves.

Barnaby flew close to my shoulder without landing on it. "I'll handle Romeo. You get that satchel and fly straight home with it."

The raven cawed and ruffled his feathers.

I ran through my options. My weapons were too dangerous. Any passerby could end up as collateral damage.

My gaze landed on a nearby fire hydrant. That would do the trick. Maintaining my invisibility, I whipped out Babe and used the axe to break open the hydrant. Water gushed from the spout and flooded the street. People scurried out of the way.

I used my elemental magic to forge a connection with the water. It swirled up into a six-foot cyclone and rotated across the pavement until it reached Romeo.

"Now, Barnaby!"

The werewolf was so distracted by the water cyclone that he failed to notice the raven. With his beak and claws, Barnaby wrenched the satchel away and took to the sky.

Romeo jumped in the air and grasped the strap of the satchel. Water splashed over him and he lost his grip. I watched with satisfaction as Barnaby flew high into the sky with the satchel.

Romeo sniffed the air, picking up my scent. "You."

I didn't give him time to act. I concentrated on the water droplets that clung to him and lowered their temperature until they froze.

Romeo advanced. Water solidified and crunched as he tried to move forward but to no avail. The werewolf was encased in a layer of ice.

I turned visible and sauntered closer to him. "Still think

you're hot stuff?" I patted the top of his head. "Might want to put that thought on ice."

At the end of the block, I noticed two vampires in uniform charging toward us. Someone had called the authorities. As much as I wanted to avoid them, I had to stay and offer a report.

"I'm London Hayes of the Knights of Boudica." I showed them my badge. "This is Romeo Rice. He's responsible for the death of one werewolf and the kidnapping of at least four more. He's pretty strong. I'd suggest getting him to a cell before the ice melts."

The vampires inspected my badge.

"And tell Prince Maeron," I added. "He'll want to know."

17

"How much did we make from the pack job?" Kami strode into my flat like she owned the place.

I closed the door behind her. "You're not going to like my answer."

Kami stooped over to pet Herman. "If the pack won't pay you for all that work, report them. That'll get their checkbook out."

"It's not that simple. Romeo hired me without pack permission. Nobody knew what he was up to. They said I should've reviewed the contract more closely."

Kami scrunched her nose. "There was a contract?"

"I'll refrain from answering that." I'd never hear the end of it from Minka either.

"The good news is that Simon said he received the funds to repair the damage to the pub, so I guess the pack decided not to be stingy with their own kind."

That *was* good news.

"You said all the werewolves were alive when you got to the rooftop?" I asked.

Kami nodded. "We kept them calm while Briar healed

their superficial wounds. Can't help with the psychological damage though."

The pack would take care of them—I hoped.

"Why are you here? You said everyone's meeting at the pub. Go enjoy the evening. You earned it dealing with those drunk centaurs."

"And so have you. Come with us," Kami urged. "Darts. Pitchers of ale. I'll even lure Minka to stand in front of the dartboard like that time in The Crown." She smacked my arm playfully. "Come on. What more could you want? It'll be a blast."

As much as I wanted to join them, to feel like part of the team, there was something more important I had to do that couldn't wait.

"Another time, I promise."

Her face drooped. "Spoilsport. You used to be fun, you know."

I smiled. "Really? I don't remember that."

She pretended to glare at me. "Yeah, you're right. You've always been a party pooper. It's why I joined the knights in the first place. To have more than one friend to throw darts with."

"I thought we did that so we could eat."

She wagged a finger at me. "Next time it'll be knives instead of darts."

"In that case I'm definitely coming and you'd better make sure to invite Minka."

She blew me a kiss and left. I closed the door and leaned against it with a weary sigh. I reset the ward, knowing there were multiple pairs of eyes burning a hole in my back.

"Patience, please," I told my furry audience. "I'll be with you in a few minutes."

Despite the ward, it wasn't safe to keep two powerful

stones in my flat. It was one thing to endanger myself; it was quite another to endanger my animal companions when they couldn't consent. I was fortunate to have another option—one that no one would guess because no one knew I was capable of such magic.

I set to work. The sooner I took care of this, the better I'd feel. I sat on the floor of my living room in the middle of a chalk circle. A trio of candles burned around me, invoking the power of three. Sandy knew better than to breach the circle. The fennec fox took one look at the setup and left the living room. Big Red scampered onto my lap and I gently set him aside.

"Sorry, buddy. No room at the inn today. I need to keep the space clear."

In typical fashion, Hera ignored me and vaulted to the bottom landing of the scratching post. I rolled my eyes and lifted her off, setting her outside the circle.

"Keep it up and you're going to force me to create a ward just so I can get through this task uninterrupted." I couldn't imagine how anyone functioned with children running around. No wonder I'd never met a knight with kids, not a female one anyway. It was dangerous enough to have people in this world you cared about, let alone your own offspring. It must've been incredibly difficult for my mother to raise me under such stressful conditions, knowing that any moment my identity might be discovered. Rhea Hayes had been tougher than I ever realized.

I glanced at the hideous green scratching post and couldn't resist a smile at my handiwork. No one would ever guess that two of the world's most powerful stones were now part of this unattractive structure. They'd fail to notice the markings. It simply looked as though I'd fashioned a scratching post out of whatever scraps I'd found and covered them with hideous green carpet.

"And now for the piece de resistance."

I made a shallow cut across my palm and sprinkled the blood around the circle. Closing my eyes, I inhaled deeply and focused on my mind's eye. No one knew the weight of the secrets I carried and that was how it had to be. They were my burden to bear.

The metaphorical lock clicked open, creating a doorway to the small realm I generally used as the menagerie's holiday home. I sent the scratching post through to the other side. Hera meowed in protest. All she saw was her chance for fun being taken away from her.

I ignored her. There were more important matters than a disgruntled cat. If Antonia was right, there were more ancient stones out there awaiting discovery and I wasn't the only one in search of them. The knowledge itself was dangerous, let alone the fact that I now possessed two of the stones and knew the location of a third. What were the other two and, more importantly, what were they capable of?

I had a lot of work to do.

I closed the doorway between worlds and unfolded my legs. It felt good to use an advanced level of magic. I rubbed away the chalk circle and blew out the candles before returning them to the shelves.

A knock startled me—mainly because it was coming from the window and not the door.

I crossed the room to the balcony and yanked open the curtains. Callan stood outside the window holding a pigeon.

My heart beat rapidly as I opened the window. "You do realize you're supposed to let the pigeon fly by itself to deliver the message?"

He smiled. "I thought this one belonged to you." He thrust the bird forward with both hands.

"You know perfectly well I work with a raven." I pointed to the sky where Barnaby was circling above. Quite frankly, I was a little annoyed the bird didn't give me a heads up about the prince's sneaky arrival. What was the point of having a protective raven if he ignored potential threats?

As though reading my thoughts, the raven cawed once and flew away.

Traitor.

"You can come in, but let the pigeon go first."

Callan released the bird and it flew away. He stooped to crawl through the window and joined me in the living room. My animal companions wisely made themselves scarce.

"Did you grab the first pigeon you saw or did they have to audition for the role of patsy?" I asked archly.

"I'll have you know Franklin is a royal pigeon. One of Davina's favorites."

"I don't think you're supposed to have favorites among your carrier pigeons."

He shrugged. "You know how she is."

I did, which was why I liked her. "What brings you here, through the proverbial back door no less?" I waved a hand at the window.

"Romeo Rice died in custody. Thought you'd want to know."

"The Tower?"

He nodded.

"What happened?"

"The report says there was an immediate fight for dominance amongst the prisoners. Mr. Rice lost."

And with him the secret of the stone. Coincidence? Maybe.

"My brother says you were responsible for apprehending Mr. Rice."

I nodded. "Another bid for power. He wanted to wrest control of the pack from bureaucrats."

"Did you find the stone?"

"Wasn't that information in the report?"

Callan looked down at the cat now threading herself between his feet. "There was no sign of any stone and Mr. Rice denied the possession of one. He said he was investigating certain pack behavior, but that he suspected it was drug-related."

"Maybe our theory was wrong then," I lied.

"My brother said he did a sweep of the penthouse but came up empty-handed." Callan must've decided resistance was futile and leaned down to pet the cat. "After everything we learned in Devon, there has to be a stone."

"Maybe not." I latched on to the idea. "Remember, the elemental stone didn't cause witches to lose control of their fire magic and burn down buildings. This could've been caused by something else." And I said a silent prayer of gratitude that it didn't have that kind of effect on me.

"*Something* had to cause the wolves here to go berserk and to relieve the condition of those in Devon."

"We'll have to keep an eye on any reports of berserkers." I decided to change the subject. I hated to lie to him, but what choice did I have? I wasn't about to hand over control of werewolves to a vampire, no matter how good of a kisser he was.

"So why didn't you come to the front door? Embarrassed to be seen with me?"

"I was being followed and I wanted to ensure no one knew my destination."

I frowned. "Who's following you? I thought your brother

was only interested in spying on my work for the pack." And that business was officially closed.

"It isn't my brother."

"Then who? Spies for Princess Louise?"

A chuckle escaped him. "Even that would be preferable."

Now I was truly stumped. "Who's worse than Louise?"

"I want you safe, London." The prince strode forward and held my face in his hands. Our lips hovered close together and I was certain he was about to kiss me.

"I am safe," I whispered.

Bright green eyes burned with regret as he released me. "This was a mistake. I shouldn't have come here."

"Why not?"

He ignored my question, taking a step backward. "I'm sorry. I have no desire to put you in danger. Stay away from me, London. Your life depends on it."

Before I could reply, the vampire transformed into a butterfly and fluttered out the window.

"Callan, wait!"

I ran to the balcony, but it was too late.

The prince was gone.

* * *

Find out what happens next in *Deadly Knight*, Book 3 in the Midnight Empire: The Tower series.

Books in the Midnight Empire: The Tower series include:

Wild Knight

Three Dog Knight

Deadly Knight

One Knight Stand

For more information about my books and to sign up for my newsletter, please visit my website at

www.annabelchase.com.

Printed in Great Britain
by Amazon